Danger in Paris

A Samantha Mystery

by Sarah Masters Buckey

Published by American Girl Publishing
Copyright © 2015 American Girl

Questions or comments? Call 1-800-845-0005,
visit **americangirl.com**, or write to Customer Service,
American Girl, 8400 Fairway Place, Middleton, WI 53562.

Printed in China
15 16 17 18 19 20 21 LEO 10 9 8 7 6 5 4 3 2 1

Cover image by Juliana Kolesova

The following individuals and organizations have given
permission to use images incorporated into the cover design:
stone interior, optimarc/Shutterstock.com; Paris scene, Jose Ignacio Soto/
Shutterstock.com; Paris catacombs, © Bertrand Rieger/Hemis/Corbis;
background pattern on back cover, © kirstypargeter/Crestock.

Cataloging-in-Publication Data available from the Library of Congress

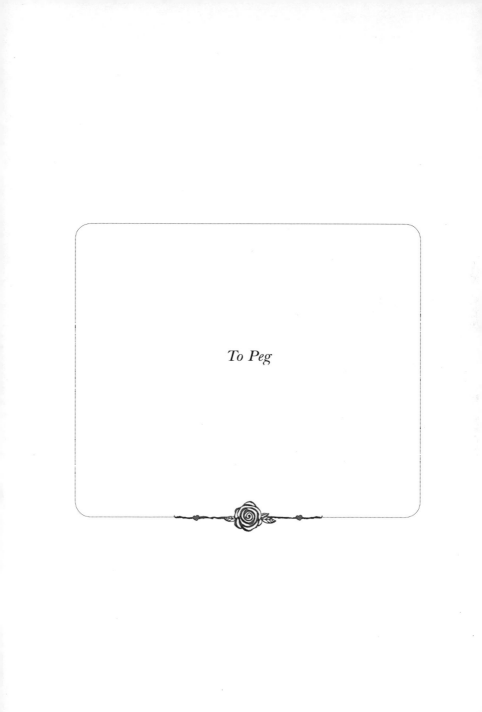

To Peg

Beforever™

The adventurous characters you'll meet in
the BeForever books will spark your curiosity
about the past, inspire you to find your voice
in the present, and excite you about your future.
You'll make friends with these girls as you share
their fun and their challenges. Like you, they are
bright and brave, imaginative and energetic,
creative and kind. Just as you are, they are
discovering what really matters: Helping others.
Being a true friend. Protecting the earth.
Standing up for what's right. Read their stories,
explore their worlds, join their adventures.
Your friendship with them will BeForever.

TABLE *of* CONTENTS

chapter 1

A Grand Adventure

LEANING OVER THE guardrail, Samantha
Parkington watched from the deck as late-arriving
passengers came aboard the ferry. The sun was setting, and the icy wind smelled of salt water. Soon
the ferry would cross the English Channel and take
them to France.

Nellie, Samantha's adopted sister and very best
friend, stood beside her, reading a pocket guide
to Paris.

"Jeepers, I know everyone speaks French in Paris,
but I didn't know so many other things were different!" Nellie pointed to the guidebook. "Samantha,
look—they have *francs* instead of dollars and *kilos*
instead of pounds. They even have a different way
to measure temperature."

"Well, however they measure it, I hope it's warmer there," said Samantha, shivering as she looked toward the harbor.

Along the wide dock, horses were pulling wagons, and a few final passengers were hurrying toward the gangplank. Samantha saw a well-dressed lady holding a wide-brimmed hat to her head, several servants toting bags, and two tall men carrying a large trunk. But there was no one who even slightly resembled Samantha and Nellie's grandfather, Admiral Archibald Beemis.

"Will the Admiral be here soon?" Nellie asked Grandmary, who was standing several feet away.

"I'm sure he will," Grandmary said briskly. She squinted into the setting sun as she kept her eyes on the dock. "We must learn to be patient, Nellie, mustn't we?"

"Yes, ma'am," said Nellie, flushing with embarrassment. She whispered to Samantha, "Did I say something wrong?"

"No, Grandmary's just worried," Samantha whispered back.

Nellie nodded, and for a moment, both girls were silent as they braced themselves against the wind. Then Nellie began to cough, the same kind of wheezing cough that had bothered her during foggy days in London. When Nellie recovered, she said in a low voice, "I'm afraid the Admiral is going to miss the ferry."

"I've never known him to be late for anything," said Samantha, scanning the shore. "He says the navy taught him to be on time."

Admiral Beemis had been born in Great Britain, and he had served for many years in the British Royal Navy. Just two years ago, he had retired and married Samantha's grandmother, who had long been a widow. Now the Admiral and Grandmary spent much of their time traveling together. This January, they had invited Samantha and Nellie on a month-long trip to Europe.

"Every young lady should visit Europe," Grandmary had told the girls. "It's an important part of
your education."

"We'll have a jolly time, too," the Admiral had
added, his blue eyes twinkling.

Samantha and Nellie had both been thrilled at the
chance to see London and Paris. Two weeks ago, they
had waved good-bye to their family in New York and
sailed across the Atlantic Ocean with the Admiral,
Grandmary, and Grandmary's elderly maid, Doris.

After an exciting week in England, they had
planned to leave London a few days ago. But the
British government had asked Admiral Beemis to
stay in London for some important meetings, so their
family had delayed their departure until today. Then
this morning, the Admiral had announced that he
had one more meeting to attend in London.

"I'll join you at the ferry this afternoon," the
Admiral had promised them. "Then we'll all travel
to Paris together."

But there was still no sign of the Admiral.

Something must be wrong, thought Samantha.

As the wind whipped her hair, Samantha heard passengers complaining that the ferry was running behind schedule. An elderly woman called to a ship's steward, "Young man, why is the ferry still here? We should have left half an hour ago."

The steward tipped his hat. "We're sorry for the delay, madam, but we've been instructed to wait for a very important passenger." The steward glanced toward the dock, where a shiny black motorcar had pulled up in front of the ferry. "Ah, it seems our passenger has arrived."

Samantha noticed a hush on deck as everyone waited for the very important passenger. In the gathering dusk, she saw the man emerge from the car. He was wearing a tall hat and carrying a gold-topped cane. He crossed the gangplank as confidently as if he'd been traveling on ships all his life.

Samantha exclaimed, "Grandmary, it's the Admiral!"

Grandmary sighed with relief. "Yes, I'm quite glad that he's here."

Samantha watched with surprise as the ferry's officers hurried out to welcome the Admiral on board. She knew that *admiral* was the highest rank in the navy, but she had always thought of Admiral Beemis as a fun and loving grandfather, not someone who was so important that a huge ferry would wait for him. But as soon as he came on board, the ferry's whistle blasted and the crew pulled up the gangplank.

"Very sorry to keep you waiting, my dears," said the Admiral as he joined them on the deck. "You must be cold. Why don't we go to the lounge?" He gestured across the deck to a door labeled in gold letters: *First-Class Passengers Only.*

Samantha and Nellie were following their grandparents toward the lounge when a woman's voice rang out nearby. "Prince! Come back here, Prince!" the woman called in a British accent. Samantha saw a slim, fashionably dressed woman clutching an empty basket.

"Is there a problem?" Grandmary asked the woman kindly.

"Oh, yes! My little dog jumped out of his basket and ran away," said the woman, looking around in distress. She seemed about the same age as Samantha's young aunt, Cornelia, but she was dressed all in black, and Samantha guessed that she was a widow. "His name is Prince—he's a small brown-and-white spaniel with a red ribbon around his neck. Have you seen him?"

Grandmary shook her head. "No, I'm sorry, but we'll keep an eye out for him."

"Thank you!" said the woman, her blue eyes brimming with tears. "I'm so afraid he'll fall overboard!"

Samantha noticed the wide gap between the

bottom of the guardrail and the deck. *If the poor dog falls overboard, he'll surely drown,* she thought. "May Nellie and I look for the dog?" she asked Grandmary.

Grandmary hesitated and then turned to the woman. "Would you like our granddaughters to help you, Mrs. . . . ?"

"Excuse me for not introducing myself." The young woman looked more flustered than ever. "I'm Mrs. Gray, and I'd certainly appreciate help. My maid, Martha, and I are going to search the upper deck. Perhaps the girls could check this deck?"

"The dog can't have gone far," said the Admiral, surveying the deck. "Girls, your grandmother and I will wait for you inside."

The deck rose and fell as the ferry headed out into wind-tossed waves. Only a few clusters of passengers remained on deck, and there weren't many places for a dog to hide.

Samantha and Nellie were searching behind empty benches along the deck when Samantha saw a flash of brown-and-white fur. She glimpsed the dog as it ran down the opposite side of the ferry. A moment later, the spaniel was blocked from view by the central cabin that held the lounge.

"Over there!" Samantha called to Nellie, and they rushed across the deck. On the other side of the ferry, they found a little boy in a blue coat and short gray trousers chasing after Prince.

"Come here, doggie!" the boy shouted in an American accent. But the tiny spaniel darted away.

"Let's wait," Samantha told the boy as she and Nellie caught up with him. "We'll follow him quietly."

The boy looked around. The dog had disappeared. "Where'd he go?"

"Under there," said Nellie, who had been keeping watch. She gestured to a long bench on the side of the ferry, just a few feet from the guardrail.

"We'll get him," Samantha told the boy. "You stay right here."

Samantha and Nellie approached the bench carefully. When Samantha peered under it, she saw the spaniel's brown eyes looking back at her from the shadows.

"Good dog!" Samantha said soothingly. She reached toward Prince, but just then the ferry rose with a wave and the deck lurched. The little dog backed away from her.

"He's scared," Samantha whispered to Nellie.

Reaching into her pocket, Nellie pulled out a handkerchief with a small wedge of cheese inside it. "Let's see if this works. I was saving it."

Samantha understood. Before being adopted, Nellie had often gone hungry. Now Nellie had plenty of food, but she couldn't stand to waste anything.

Nellie held out the cheese to Prince. "It's cheddar," she coaxed him.

The small dog edged closer. His button nose quivered as he sniffed the cheese. Finally, he stepped forward, and Samantha grasped the red silk ribbon around his neck.

"Got him!" she declared. She picked up Prince and noticed that his fur was damp. "You must be freezing," she said, nestling him in her arms.

Nellie fed him the cheese. Prince gulped it down, as if he hadn't eaten in days. Then he wagged his tail, his whole body wriggling with happiness.

As Samantha carried Prince to the waiting boy, a plump young woman with light blonde hair, round glasses, and sensible black shoes ran up to them. "Bertie!" she burst out. "You *must* stop running away!"

"I found a dog, Ingrid!" said Bertie as he patted the spaniel in Samantha's arms.

Samantha and Nellie introduced themselves, and Ingrid explained that she was Bertie's nanny. "I'd better get him back to the lounge," she added with an apologetic smile. "His parents just sat down to tea."

They all walked toward the first-class lounge together and entered it through a set of double doors.

Inside, passengers were chatting and having tea, scones, and sandwiches at linen-covered tables. As soon as they walked in, Mrs. Gray hurried over and scooped Prince into her arms. "Thank heavens you girls found him!" she exclaimed, stroking the dog's silky head.

"Bertie was the first to spot him," Samantha said, and Bertie grinned proudly.

Samantha and Nellie saw the Admiral and Grandmary at a corner table. The Admiral, standing up politely, invited Mrs. Gray to join them, too.

Bertie's parents were seated at the next table, and they introduced themselves as Mr. and Mrs. Robert Vanderhoff from Buffalo, New York. "I own Vanderhoff's Mills," Mr. Vanderhoff volunteered. He was a big man with a double chin and a thick gold watch chain that stretched across his stomach. "Perhaps you've heard of us? We produce the finest wheat flour in New York!"

Mrs. Gray held Prince in her lap and sat down

next to Samantha. "It was so kind of your grand-daughters to find Prince for me," she told Grandmary. "I'd like to send them each a note of thanks when I get to Paris."

"There's no need to do that," said Grandmary, passing a platter of triangle-shaped sandwiches around the table. "I'm sure the girls were happy to assist you."

As Samantha helped herself to sandwiches, she felt something touch her arm. It was Prince's paw. He was nudging her hopefully.

Samantha couldn't resist the spaniel's pleading eyes. She checked to be sure no one was watching. Then she passed Prince a ham sandwich under the tablecloth.

"No, I insist on thanking your granddaughters," Mrs. Gray was saying to Grandmary and the Admiral. "Since my dear husband's death, Prince is the only family I have left. I would've been heartbroken to lose him." Mrs. Gray glanced over at Samantha and

Nellie, and a smile brightened her delicate features. "So I must write you girls proper thank-you notes. What will your address be in France?"

"We shall be at the Imperial Excelsior Hotel in Paris," said Grandmary. "Do you know it?"

"The Imperial Excelsior!" Mrs. Gray's eyebrows shot up. "Why, that's where I'll be staying!"

"What a coincidence! We're staying there, too!" boomed Mr. Vanderhoff from the next table.

"We've heard it's really the *finest* hotel in Paris," chimed in Mrs. Vanderhoff, a dark-haired, birdlike woman with a gleaming string of pearls around her neck. "Our banker recommended it."

Mrs. Vanderhoff lowered her voice confidentially. "Our banker also warned us that there are gangs of thieves in Paris," she continued. "That's why we signed up for the Imperial Excelsior's guided tours of the city."

Samantha was about to bite into a cucumber sandwich, but she paused, the sandwich halfway to her mouth. *Paris has gangs of thieves? The guidebook didn't mention that.*

Mrs. Gray's eyes widened. "Oh dear! All my life I've dreamed of visiting Paris. I never imagined it would be dangerous. And now that my husband is gone, I'm traveling with only Martha, my maid . . ."

"Well, you should sign up for the guided tour," advised Mrs. Vanderhoff. Barely pausing to catch her breath, she told frightening tales of tourists who had been robbed in Paris. "They call it 'The City of Light,' but there's a dark side to Paris," Mrs. Vanderhoff concluded with a knowing smile. "Our friends in Buffalo told us all about it!"

Samantha put down her sandwich. Suddenly she was no longer hungry. She glanced over and saw Nellie staring fixedly at her plate. Samantha wondered whether Nellie was scared, too.

The Admiral said, "I've been to Paris many times. It's a beautiful city, and I've never had a problem. The Imperial Excelsior Hotel should be quite safe, too. It's one of the biggest hotels, and travelers from all over the world stay there."

"That's reassuring," sighed Mrs. Gray. "You see, I was born in England, but I've spent most of my life in Australia, and I don't know much about Europe." Her face looked pale as she turned to Grandmary. "Mrs. Beemis, do *you* think it would be wise to sign up for the hotel's tour? Will you and your grand-daughters be taking it?"

"Our friends tell us it's the best way to see the city," urged Mr. Vanderhoff. He leaned back in his chair, one thumb hooked in his watch chain. "I hate to wait anywhere. Efficiency, that's my motto! With the tour there's no standing in line for tickets, either. The tour guide will even arrange opera tickets for the evenings."

"It does sound quite convenient," Grandmary said thoughtfully.

Nellie started coughing, and Grandmary reached for the teapot. "Have something hot to drink, Nellie," she said, pouring her a steaming cup. "Mrs. Gray, would you care for tea?"

The ferry rose and fell again, and Mrs. Gray gripped the table with one hand. Clasping Prince in her other arm, she stood up unsteadily. "Please excuse me," she said. "I'm afraid I suffer from seasickness. I must go take my pills."

As Mrs. Gray hurried away, Samantha remembered that Nellie often got seasick, too. "Are you all right?" she asked her sister in a low voice.

"I think so," said Nellie without looking up. "But no sandwiches, thank you."

Just then, the ferry lurched. Dishes clattered and the lamps flickered. A cloud of concern passed over Grandmary's face.

But the Admiral sipped his tea calmly. "This is just a bit of rough sea. It won't be long till we arrive in France. And then Paris will be a grand adventure!"

chapter 2

The Red-Haired Man's Warning

BY THE TIME the ferry reached the coast of
France, the sky was black and the wind was blowing
the sea into frothy waves. The girls and their grandparents and Grandmary's maid, Doris, all stopped for
the night at an inn in the coastal town.

The next morning, cold rain poured down as
they traveled by train to Paris. Sitting in their train
compartment, Samantha and Nellie played a game
of guessing what the French signs meant.

"Look, Samantha," cried Nellie, jumping up and
pointing out the window at a sign that said *Paris 50K.*
"I bet that's for kilometers!"

Grandmary glanced up from her needlework.
"Please remember that it's not polite to point, Nellie,"
she said quietly but firmly. "And, as my governess

always told me, a proper young lady never raises her voice unless there's some sort of danger, such as a house on fire."

"Yes, ma'am," said Nellie, blushing. She sat down again, folding her hands in her lap.

Watching Grandmary and Nellie sit silently across from each other, Samantha wished she could reach out her hands to them both. Samantha's own parents had died when she was little, and she had lived with Grandmary before being adopted by her Uncle Gard and Aunt Cornelia in New York City. She loved her grandmother very much and knew that, although Grandmary was strict and dignified, she had a kind and loving heart.

But Samantha also knew that Nellie was in awe of Grandmary. "Your grandmother is very nice, but she's just the way I'd always imagined a queen would be," Nellie had once told Samantha.

Nellie's parents had been poor immigrants, and as a small child Nellie had helped her family by working first in a factory and later as a servant. Nellie had been working as a maid when she and Samantha met. Despite the fact that Samantha's family was wealthy and Nellie's was poor, the two girls had become best friends. After Nellie's parents had died of influenza, ten-year-old Nellie and her younger sisters, Bridget and Jenny, had lived in a terrible orphanage until Samantha and Aunt Cornelia had rescued them.

One of the happiest days of Samantha's life had been when Aunt Cornelia and Uncle Gard had decided to adopt Nellie, Bridget, and Jenny. Samantha now had the big family she'd always longed for, but she knew that Nellie sometimes felt out of place among her new relatives.

If only there was some way I could help, thought Samantha as the train sped through the French countryside.

The Admiral looked up from his newspaper. "You're right about the sign, Nellie," he said, smiling.

"And if we're only fifty kilometers from Paris, we should arrive in less than an hour."

Samantha and Nellie excused themselves to go wash up. As they walked along the narrow train aisle, Nellie confided, "Samantha, I'm not sure I'll ever learn to be a proper young lady. I try hard, but I always forget something!"

"I forget things, too," said Samantha. "But Grandmary says that young ladies were *always* well-behaved when she was a girl. Can you imagine?"

Nellie shook her head. "No, I can't," she said solemnly as the train rattled down the track.

When they arrived in Paris, a hired carriage took them to the hotel. The air was still very cold, but the sun was shining now and there were only a few puffs of clouds in the blue sky. As they rode through the streets, Samantha saw bakeries displaying long golden loaves of bread, men in berets bicycling fast, and fashionable ladies walking dogs. The pets wore ribbons around their necks and colorful jackets.

"Even the dogs wear fancy clothes here!" Samantha whispered to Nellie.

Nellie coughed into her lace handkerchief. Then she peered eagerly out the window. "I can hardly wait to write to Bridget and Jenny. I want to tell them all about Paris."

The carriage stopped in front of the Imperial Excelsior Hotel, a regal-looking stone building set on a busy street. It was past lunchtime, and Samantha's stomach was grumbling. But she forgot her hunger as she walked into the hotel. Sun streamed in through the lobby's windows, and everything shone brightly, from the gilt-framed mirrors on the walls to the brass buttons on the hotel staff's uniforms. Even the black-and-white marble floor gleamed.

Travelers in well-tailored coats and fashionable hats were lined up at the registration desk, waiting to check into their rooms. "It's quite busy, especially for January," said Grandmary, looking around.

A portly man with a large mustache hurried out

to greet them. "Welcome to Paris, Admiral Beemis,"
he said in perfect English. He bowed formally.
"I am Monsieur Andreyev, manager of the Imperial
Excelsior. The British Embassy told us you were
arriving, and we saved one of our finest suites for
you. I'll take you there myself!"

As the manager ushered them to the elevator, he
pointed out the hotel's luxurious lounges and a reading room with books in many languages. Then he
gestured toward a dining room with crystal chandeliers. "And our restaurant is famous!" he added.

Samantha noticed that people in the lobby were
staring at them, as if wondering why they got such
special treatment. She grew hot with embarrassment.
I guess the Admiral really is important, she thought.

Nellie suddenly said, "There's Mrs. Gray and
Prince!" She held up her hand to point but then
quickly put it down again.

Samantha looked over and saw Mrs. Gray standing in line at the registration desk. Martha was

holding Prince, and the spaniel was now wearing a blue bow and matching jacket. "He already looks like a French dog," Samantha whispered to Nellie.

Monsieur Andreyev said something in French to the uniformed man operating the elevator. Samantha caught a word that sounded something like *quatre*, the French word for "four." She smiled to herself when the elevator took them to the fourth floor, the highest floor of the hotel. *At least I understand a little French*, she thought.

She and her family followed Monsieur Andreyev down a carpeted hallway. "Here is your suite," he said, opening the door to Suite 401 and escorting them into the marble-tiled entryway.

Looking around, Samantha thought, *It's more like a fancy apartment than a hotel!*

To the right of the entryway, a short hall led to a doorway. "There's the servant's bedroom," said Monsieur Andreyev. "It has an ironing board and the latest conveniences." Doris looked impressed.

Monsieur Andreyev then ushered them straight
ahead, into a sunny sitting room with large windows
framed by white curtains. A butter-yellow sofa and
two matching armchairs faced the fireplace, where
a cozy fire was burning. An antique clock ticked on
the mantel.

Samantha saw a polished dining table and a spin-
dly legged writing desk across the room. Monsieur
Andreyev pointed out the shiny black telephone that
perched on the desk like a tall bird.

"We are among the first hotels in the world to
have telephones for our guests," he said proudly.
"Just click the receiver, and the clerk at the front desk
will answer."

There were three doors off the sitting room.
One led to a large bedroom for Grandmary and the
Admiral, another opened to a white-tiled bathroom
with an enormous bathtub, and the third led to
Samantha and Nellie's bedroom, a pretty room with
twin beds and yellow-and-blue-flowered wallpaper.

Once Monsieur Andreyev had left, Samantha and Nellie settled into their room. Sun was shining through big windows that overlooked the city. Samantha sighed with happiness as she plopped down on her twin bed. "I like it here, Nellie!"

"Me too!" Nellie agreed, stretching out on her own bed.

But as they unpacked, Samantha's stomach began to growl. She was glad when the Admiral announced that they would eat lunch in the hotel restaurant. After lunch, Grandmary returned to the suite to rest, but the Admiral, Samantha, and Nellie set out for a stroll.

As soon as they stepped out into the frosty air, the sights and sounds of Paris surrounded them. Walking quickly to stay warm, they passed a fruit seller calling out in French, businessmen in top hats striding fast, and ancient-looking buildings flying foreign flags. After a few blocks, they saw an enormous stone arch towering over a circle in the middle of traffic.

"That's the *Arc de Triomphe,* or Arch of Triumph,"

said the Admiral. "The French emperor, Napoleon, built it to celebrate his battle victories."

He guided Nellie and Samantha through the busy traffic to the circle, where the Arc de Triomphe loomed above them. Broad boulevards radiated from the circle like the spokes of an immense wheel. Everywhere Samantha turned, motorcars and horse-drawn carriages clattered on the boulevards around her. "I feel as if I'm at the center of the world," she said, looking out from underneath the arch.

"Not too long ago, Paris *was* the center of the French empire," said the Admiral. "Napoleon's empire stretched around the world."

"What do all these carvings mean?" Nellie asked.

Samantha turned and saw her sister examining the arch's carved stone blocks. There were several tourists behind Nellie, and Samantha thought that two tall men in the group looked familiar. One of the men was pale and very thin, and he was staring at the Admiral. But when the Admiral stepped closer to Nellie, the man turned away, as if he didn't want to be noticed.

"The carvings remind us of wars from the past, and the soldiers who died in them," said the Admiral, reaching out to touch the names carved in stone. "Let's hope there is never another war in Europe."

The Admiral turned and gestured toward a wide boulevard. "The *Champs-Élysées* is one of the most famous avenues in the world—why don't we explore it?"

As they strolled past shops and restaurants, the Admiral stopped at a kiosk and bought two newspapers, one in French and one in English. Then he asked if Samantha and Nellie would like to buy gifts to send home.

"We'd love to!" said Samantha, and Nellie nodded eagerly.

Samantha almost forgot the cold as she and Nellie looked into all the brightly lit shop windows, searching for just the right gifts. Finally they paused at a shop with a pink-striped awning. The shop window displayed chess sets and toys, pretty parasols, and, in the center, a finely crafted replica of Paris's famous Eiffel Tower. The model was about three feet tall and highly polished.

"Isn't that tower beautiful?" Nellie leaned so close that her breath made a cloud of fog on the window.

"Let's go inside," Samantha urged.

A bell tinkled as they entered the shop. The Admiral talked to a young salesclerk in French, and the clerk lifted the metal tower out of the display. She turned the model around and showed them two small drawers half-hidden in its base.

"This would be perfect for Bridget and Jenny's room! They could put jewelry and ribbons in the little drawers!" said Nellie, touching the polished metal. Then she looked at the tag, where the price was in francs. "I don't know how much this costs in American money. Is it too expensive, Admiral?"

The Admiral glanced at the tag and raised his eyebrows. Then he looked at Nellie and Samantha and smiled. "If your sisters would like it, let's buy it."

In the same store, the girls found a flowered parasol with an ebony handle for Aunt Cornelia and, for Uncle Gard, a heavy walking stick with a hidden compartment inside that stored an umbrella. They also picked out lots of postcards to send to family and friends.

When they'd finished, the Admiral spoke in French with the clerk. Samantha tried to understand what he was saying, but she caught only a few words.

In France, people speak a lot faster than my French teacher does in school, she thought, frustrated.

After he paid the clerk with strange-looking French money, the Admiral put the postcards in his suit pocket and arranged to have the gifts delivered to their hotel. "Now let's walk a little farther," he said. "I want to surprise your grandmother with her favorite candies."

The sky was growing dark, and as they walked Samantha remembered Mrs. Vanderhoff's warnings about thieves. She glanced around uneasily. Everyone around her seemed to be shopping or working, and no one seemed threatening at all. But Samantha did notice that the two men she'd seen earlier at the Arc de Triomphe were now walking along the Champs-Élysées.

Maybe all tourists come here, she thought.

The Admiral led the way to a closet-sized shop labeled *Chocolatier.* Inside, Samantha breathed in the heavenly aroma of chocolate. The Admiral bought two small bags of chocolate squares wrapped in shiny papers. He handed each girl a bag.

"You may each have one candy now, but save the rest for after dinner," he said with a smile.

As the Admiral talked to the man behind the counter, Samantha quickly unwrapped one of her squares and took a bite. "Mmm, delicious!" she declared.

Nellie sampled one of her chocolates and then nodded. "It's the best chocolate I've ever had."

In careful English, the man behind the counter

explained that he didn't make the type of chocolates that the Admiral was looking for. The man reached into his apron and then wrote an address on a slip of paper. "You may wish to try the shop at this address—*14, rue du Jardin*," he said, handing the Admiral the paper.

The Admiral thanked him and pocketed the address.

"I will go there tomorrow," he told the girls as they stepped out of the warm shop and back to the cold, windy street. "But don't tell your grandmother. I want to surprise her!"

By the time they reached the Imperial Excelsior Hotel, Nellie had started coughing again. The Admiral offered her an extra handkerchief and asked if she was ill.

"I'm fine, sir, really," Nellie told him quickly.

Monsieur Andreyev stepped from behind the registration desk when they entered the lobby. "Sir, a note for you arrived today from the Russian Embassy."

He presented the Admiral with an envelope sealed
with red wax. Then he lowered his voice. "I myself
am from Russia. If I can help you with anything,
please let me know."

*Why would the Russian Embassy send the Admiral
a note?* Samantha wondered as the Admiral tucked
the note into his suit pocket.

"Also, a gentleman from the British Embassy
is waiting for you in the reading room," the hotel
manager continued.

"Thank you, monsieur," said the Admiral. He
turned to Samantha and Nellie. "You girls go up to
our suite. I'll join you shortly."

As Samantha and Nellie headed for the elevator,
Nellie had another bout of coughing. When she recovered she said, "Let's write postcards as soon as we get
upstairs. That way, we can send them tomorrow."

"Good idea," said Samantha. Then she stopped
short. "Wait! The Admiral has the postcards in his
pocket. I'll get them and meet you upstairs."

As Nellie stepped onto the elevator, Samantha headed to the reading room. She opened the heavy wooden door quietly, so as not to disturb anyone. Inside, the long room was like a library. The walls were lined floor to ceiling with books, and there were several leather armchairs.

But the room was empty except for the Admiral and a thin, red-haired man dressed in a black suit. The two men were standing about twenty feet away and talking intently, with their backs to the door.

Samantha paused by a shoulder-high bookcase. She thought, *Maybe I should come back later.*

Then she heard the red-haired man say, "Sir, the British ambassador told me to warn you that you may be in great danger."

The Admiral is in danger? Samantha felt a chill all over. She ducked down, as if reaching for a book on the lowest shelf, and listened intently.

chapter 3

Secrets in the Reading Room

CROUCHING IN THE shadow of the bookcase, Samantha heard her grandfather say, "I appreciate the warning, but I know how important this letter is to Great Britain. I'm meeting with the Russian ambassador tomorrow, and I hope I can convince him to sign the letter."

"The Germans and their allies are watching what's happening in London, and they may know that you're carrying a secret letter, Admiral," the red-haired man cautioned. "These countries will want to know what's in the letter. Some people might even try to steal it. Be on your guard at all times. Trust no one!"

"I'll be careful," the Admiral agreed. "And after the Russians sign the letter, I'll deliver it personally to the British ambassador. I won't entrust it to anyone else."

35

The red-haired man and the Admiral started walking toward the door together. Samantha heard them pass by on the other side of the shelves, and she crouched low so that they wouldn't see her.

After the men went by, Samantha peeked over the bookcase. She saw the red-haired man shake hands with the Admiral and then walk out the door.

As her grandfather was about to leave, too, Samantha stood up. "Admiral?"

He whirled around. "Samantha! What are you doing here?"

Samantha slowly stepped out from behind the bookcase. "I heard what that man said. Are you really in danger?"

"You shouldn't listen to other people's conversations, Samantha," said the Admiral sternly. "It's not polite—and often you'll misunderstand what they are saying."

"I didn't mean to listen, not at first anyway," Samantha admitted. "I just came to get the postcards."

She looked up at her grandfather. "Then I heard that
red-haired man talking, and I was afraid for you."

"You mustn't worry," the Admiral reassured her.
He glanced around the reading room and then said
quietly, "That gentleman and I were just discuss-
ing a letter that the British government has asked
me to deliver to the Russian ambassador in Paris.
We hope the Russians will sign this letter tomorrow.
Afterward, I'll personally hand the letter to the British
ambassador." The Admiral patted her shoulder. "Then
I'll be done, and we'll all enjoy our holiday."

"But why do *you* have to deliver the letter?"
Samantha asked. "Couldn't they send it by mail?"

"I've been asked to talk to the Russian ambassador
because I've known him for a long time," the Admiral
explained. He paused and then added, "This is an
important letter, Samantha. It is part of what we hope
will someday be a larger agreement that will help
keep peace in Europe. But this letter must stay secret."

"Why?"

The Admiral frowned, etching lines in his forehead. "It's possible that some people in Germany or elsewhere in Europe might go to great lengths to discover what's in the letter—and perhaps try to stop it from being signed." He looked very serious. "Your grandmother knows about my mission here, but no one else must know about it—or about the letter. Do you understand?"

Samantha took a deep breath, smelling the leather-bound volumes that filled the room. "I understand."

"Good. Now, let's go upstairs," said the Admiral, smiling again. "Your grandmother and I are going to the opera tonight."

After dinner, Grandmary and the Admiral left for the opera, saying that they would be back very late. Samantha and Nellie went to their room and looked through the gifts they had purchased.

The gifts had been delivered to the hotel in a large

crate, and the Admiral had said that he'd have the crate shipped to New York the next day. As light from their bedside lamps cast shadows on the wall, Nellie unwrapped the brown paper that surrounded the replica of the Eiffel Tower. Then she tucked postcards into the tower's hidden drawers.

Samantha took out crayons and paper that she'd brought along on the trip. She wrote on the paper in red letters:

SECRET
DO NOT OPEN UNTIL WE GET BACK!

She showed the note to Nellie. "I was going to put this on top of the Eiffel Tower. Do you think it will work?"

"Maybe," said Nellie. "But Bridget and Jenny might sneak a peek anyway. They are *awfully* curious."

"You're right," Samantha agreed. At the bottom of the note, she wrote: **PLEASE WAIT FOR US!**

"I can hardly wait to see Bridget and Jenny again," said Nellie, looking down at the crate.

"Me too!" Samantha agreed. But she knew that the wait was even harder for Nellie, who missed her younger sisters terribly.

"We'll be home soon after the gifts arrive," Samantha reminded her.

"Yes," Nellie agreed. "But—" Before she could finish her sentence, she had another fit of coughing.

Doris knocked and then came into the bedroom carrying the girls' freshly ironed dresses. "Your cough sounds bad, Nellie," Doris declared. She was hard of hearing, and she always spoke loudly. "Your grandmother says a hot bath might make it better. You should go take a long soak."

Nellie got up to take her bath, and after she was finished, it was Samantha's turn. As Samantha soaked in the big white claw-footed tub, she thought about the Admiral's secret letter. She knew that her grandfather was very brave, and she wondered whether he was really in more danger than he admitted.

She wished she'd asked the Admiral if she could tell Nellie about the letter. *I'll ask him tomorrow,* she decided.

Samantha stayed in the tub so long that her fingers and toes looked as shriveled as raisins. When she finally got out, she found that Nellie had fallen asleep in their room. Samantha tiptoed into the bedroom and picked up her Sherlock Holmes book and her bag of delicious chocolates. Doris had gone to bed, and the suite was quiet. Snuggled on the couch in her warm bathrobe, Samantha unwrapped a square of chocolate and munched while she turned the pages of the detective stories.

One piece of chocolate led to another, and Samantha soon realized the bag was empty. *I'll just read for a few more minutes,* she thought.

But she must have fallen asleep, because the next thing she knew, she was awakened by a knock on the door. She sat up on the couch, her heart pounding.

"Hello?" she called loudly. She glanced at the clock on the mantel. It was almost eleven-thirty.

"I have the tray of food you ordered," said a quiet voice.

Samantha stood up and was about to unlock the door when a tingle of worry stopped her. She remembered what the red-haired man had said: *Trust no one.*

"We already had dinner," Samantha called through the door. "I think you have the wrong room."

There was no answer, just the light rustle of footsteps moving away. After a few moments, Samantha knelt down and looked through the crack beneath the door. She saw light from the hall, but no sign of anyone standing there.

The hotel must have made a mistake, Samantha told herself as she stood up again. But she had a strange feeling that something was wrong, and she made sure the door was firmly locked. Then she wrapped her bathrobe tightly around herself and went to bed.

chapter 4
The Spyglass

THE NEXT MORNING, Samantha and Nellie were sipping hot chocolate and eating flaky *croissants* when the Admiral and Grandmary came into the sunny sitting room. The Admiral was wearing his best black suit and carrying his leather briefcase and gold-topped walking stick.

"It's all arranged that your grandmother and you girls will take the tour today, and I shall join you later," he said cheerfully. "I hope you enjoy the sights!"

"And I hope everything goes well with your meeting, dear," Grandmary told him as she brushed a speck of dust off his suit and straightened the collar of his topcoat. "Do you have the papers you need?"

"Yes," said the Admiral, patting the breast pocket

of his suit coat. "And I have the schedule of the tour—
I will try to join you at the Eiffel Tower."

When the door closed behind the Admiral, a look
of worry passed over Grandmary's face. Then she said
briskly, "Girls, the tour meets in the hotel lobby at
nine o'clock, so please finish breakfast and get ready."

They arrived in the lobby at ten minutes before
nine. As Grandmary paused at the hotel desk,
Samantha and Nellie went to talk to Mrs. Gray, who
was sitting in an armchair with Prince on her lap.
The widow looked fashionable in a black traveling suit and wide-brimmed black hat topped with
feathers. Martha stood silently beside Mrs. Gray.
The maid was a heavyset young woman with dark
blonde hair pulled into a tight bun. She pursed her
lips disapprovingly when Prince yipped at Samantha
and Nellie.

Mrs. Gray greeted the girls warmly. "I saw
Admiral Beemis leaving a short while ago," she noted.
"Isn't your grandfather coming with us this morning?"

"No," said Samantha, patting Prince, who was wearing a green jacket and matching bow. "The Admiral has a meeting this morning."

As soon as the words were out of her mouth, Samantha wished she'd been more careful. *The Admiral said no one should know about his mission!*

But Mrs. Gray just nodded. "Well, it must be an important meeting for the Admiral to miss the tour." Then, as Grandmary joined them, she added, "Ah, Mrs. Beemis, how nice to see you again!"

A pair of tall, square-jawed young men entered the lobby together. They were both wearing dark suits and homburg hats, but one man looked hearty and athletic, while the other was pale and very thin. Samantha realized that they were the same two men she'd seen yesterday.

The thin man approached Grandmary. Lifting his hat, he bowed awkwardly. "Pardon me, ma'am, my name is Frederick Keller. I'm from Toronto, Canada. And . . ." He hesitated. "Well, I wondered if by any chance you are related to Admiral Archibald Beemis, the brilliant admiral who modernized the Royal Navy?"

Samantha was surprised by the young man's question. Grandmary always said that ladies should not talk to strangers unless they had been properly introduced. Now Samantha waited to see how her grandmother would respond.

Grandmary nodded curtly to the man. "Yes, Mr. Keller. Admiral Beemis is my husband, but he is now retired from the navy."

"Please, call me Frederick," the young man said eagerly. He didn't seem to notice Grandmary's reserved manner. "My cousin and I are taking this tour. Will the Admiral be on it, too?"

"He shall join us later," Grandmary replied frostily.

Frederick's pale face flushed with enthusiasm. "I've read a great deal about Admiral Beemis, and I'd be honored to meet him!" Frederick exclaimed. He

added that he was a history teacher, and he'd always
been fascinated by naval history.

"Well, I'm sure you'll have a chance to talk with
the Admiral," said Grandmary, a bit more cordially.

Frederick introduced himself to Mrs. Gray,
Samantha, and Nellie. Then he gestured to the man
standing beside him. "This is my cousin, William
Keller. He's from Toronto, too, and he's a—"

"Geologist," William interrupted. A smile flitted
across his face. "I study rocks, so both my cousin and
I learn history. But what I study is a lot older."

Frederick looked surprised by William's comment. But he didn't say anything, and as she watched
the two men talk with Grandmary, Samantha suddenly remembered where she had first seen them.
The men had been among the last passengers to
board the ferry. She'd noticed them because they had
walked on carrying a trunk between them.

I guess it's a coincidence that we keep running into
them, she thought.

A clock began to chime, and Mr. and Mrs. Vanderhoff hurried into the lobby, with Ingrid and Bertie trailing behind them. "Where is that blasted tour guide?" demanded Mr. Vanderhoff. "He said we'd start at nine!"

Before the final chime sounded, a small, very neatly dressed man walked briskly up to the group, his boots clicking on the marble floor. His carefully combed hair and trimmed beard were just beginning to turn gray, but his brown eyes sparkled with energy.

"I am Monsieur LeBlanc, owner of LeBlanc's Paris Tours," he announced in perfect English. Then he smiled. "I look forward to showing you my beautiful city. Please follow me!"

Monsieur LeBlanc ushered them into his omnibus, a large carriage pulled by a team of horses. He gave a command to the driver, and they set off through Paris. Monsieur LeBlanc pointed out famous sights as they rode along. Samantha enjoyed listening to the guide as he shared tidbits of history and talked about kings and queens from centuries ago as if they were his old friends.

They stopped for lunch at a café that smelled tantalizingly of spices. As they all sat together at a long wooden table, Samantha and Nellie struggled with the menu. Grandmary, who spoke fluent French, helped them order roast chicken and crispy fried potatoes called *pommes frites*.

"I wish I could read this," said Ingrid, studying her menu. "All I know is English and some German from my parents."

"William and I learned German from our parents, too!" said Frederick from across the table. As the three of them began speaking German together, Monsieur LeBlanc joined them in fluent German.

Samantha remembered the red-haired man's warning. He'd said that the Germans might know about the secret letter. *But it's probably just another coincidence that so many people on the tour speak German*, she thought.

"I only know English," Mrs. Gray said
apologetically.

"Well, English is good enough for us!" said Mr.
Vanderhoff. He pointed a blunt finger at the menu.
"I'll take that," he told the waiter.

Samantha noticed a plate of cream-filled desserts
on the next table. She tried to remember the right
word in French. Finally she ventured, *"Une pâtisserie,
s'il vous plaît,* Grandmary?"

"I'm glad you're trying to speak the language,
Samantha," Grandmary said approvingly. "Would
you like a pastry, too, Nellie?"

Nellie's eyes lit up. "Yes, please!" Then she cor-
rected herself. "I mean, s'il vous plaît."

"Very good, Nellie," said Grandmary. Nellie
beamed, and Grandmary ordered desserts for
both girls.

After lunch, they climbed back into the omnibus. As the horses clip-clopped down the street,
Monsieur LeBlanc leaned forward in his seat. "Next,

we shall climb *la tour Eiffel,* one of the most famous sites in Paris."

"Samantha, look—there it is!" said Nellie, forgetting for a moment Grandmary's rules about pointing.

Samantha peered past her sister. "Jiminy!" she gasped. "It's huge!" The Eiffel Tower's four massive supports rose from the earth like the legs of giants. Samantha had to crane her neck to see the top of the huge metal tower.

"Oh dear!" said Mrs. Gray. "There *are* elevators we can take instead of climbing stairs, aren't there, Monsieur LeBlanc?"

"Unfortunately, *madame,* only elevators to the first level are working today. But there's a restaurant on that level. Perhaps you could wait there while others climb to the second level?"

"That's an excellent idea," said Mrs. Gray. She turned to her maid. "Martha, please walk Prince around the grounds. And keep him on his leash.

We don't want him to run away today, do we?"

Martha scowled at the dog on her lap. She looked as if she wished Prince would run away forever. But all she said was, "Yes, ma'am."

Monsieur LeBlanc guided the group to one of the tower's metal-cage elevators. Crammed in with dozens of tourists, Samantha was squeezed so tightly behind Frederick that all she could see was his hat and his dark, very thick hair. As the elevator creaked upward, Monsieur LeBlanc told them, "This is the world's tallest building. Thousands of people visit each year. Soon you will see why."

The elevator groaned to a stop, and everyone piled out. Samantha saw visitors strolling along the tower's metal walkways, sipping coffee at a restaurant with wide windows, and shopping for souvenirs. For a moment, she almost forgot how high up they were.

Then she turned and peered over the railing. Suddenly she felt queasy. The trees and motorcars were so far away, they looked tiny.

But Monsieur LeBlanc gestured to a metal staircase. "It's only three hundred and eighty steps to the next level. And the view is *magnifique!*"

"I'd love to see it!" Ingrid volunteered excitedly, and Bertie agreed.

"I'll stay in the restaurant," Mrs. Gray declared. "Mrs. Beemis, will you join me?"

"Yes. My husband said he'd meet us at the Eiffel Tower, so I'll wait for him on this level," Grandmary said. She smiled at Samantha and Nellie. "You girls may climb the stairs if you wish."

"Thank you, ma'am, I'd like to!" said Nellie happily.

Samantha swallowed hard. She was secretly nervous about climbing higher, but she didn't want to spoil Nellie's fun. "I'll go with you," she said.

Bertie convinced his father to come along, but Mrs. Vanderhoff said that she would wait at the restaurant with the other ladies.

"I'll stay at the restaurant, too," said Frederick.

"I would've thought a young fellow like you wouldn't be afraid to climb a few steps," Mr. Vanderhoff teased him.

Frederick frowned. "I'm tired today. I want to rest."

William shot a dark look at Mr. Vanderhoff and then turned to Fredrick. He said encouragingly, "Yes, stay here, Fred. I'll go up and tell you what it's like."

As Samantha followed Nellie up the stairs, she wondered why William didn't want Frederick to climb the tower. She recalled that both cousins spoke German, and Frederick had been awfully eager to ask questions about the Admiral. She couldn't shake her suspicion that there was something odd about the cousins.

Maybe I'm just imagining things, she told herself as she climbed the open metalwork staircase. The wind tossed her hair and looking down made her stomach turn, so she kept her eyes focused straight ahead as they climbed. And climbed . . .

Finally, they reached the second level. Most of the

group gathered by the railing and looked out. But Samantha stayed a few feet back from the others.

It really is a beautiful view, she thought, gazing out at the River Seine and the city of Paris stretching for miles around her. *I just can't look straight down!*

Monsieur LeBlanc took an old-fashioned spyglass from his knapsack and passed it around. One by one, members of the group peered through the spyglass and marveled at how far they could see.

"Come join us," Monsieur LeBlanc urged Samantha. As he offered her the spyglass, the others turned to look at her.

Samantha didn't want to go anywhere near the railing, but Nellie came over and said quietly, "I'll stay right next to you."

With Nellie beside her, Samantha stepped forward and held the cold metal spyglass to her eye. At first, everything looked blurry. Then she adjusted the focus and could see tourists on the ground below. A white-haired man wearing a black coat and top hat and carrying a gold-topped walking stick came into view.

"The Admiral's here!" she told Nellie. Samantha felt a rush of relief. As she saw her grandfather walk confidently toward the tower, she felt sure that his secret mission at the Russian Embassy had been successful. *Thank heavens it's over,* she thought.

While she watched her grandfather, Samantha was surprised to see Frederick come into view. The tall Canadian tipped his hat to the Admiral as if introducing himself. Then he and the Admiral walked toward the tower together.

Frederick said he wanted to rest, Samantha recalled. *Why is he out walking?*

Samantha felt a tug on her arm. It was Bertie. "Can I look through it again?"

"Oh, yes," said Samantha, handing the little boy the spyglass.

Soon it was time to go back down the metal stairs. As the group gathered in the restaurant, Monsieur LeBlanc took a camera from his knapsack and asked them to stand together for a photograph. Samantha noticed that Frederick positioned himself right next to the Admiral and Grandmary. Samantha and Nellie had to wedge themselves in beside their grandparents. *I wish Frederick would go stand with his cousin instead,* thought Samantha.

The camera clicked, and everyone relaxed. Then Monsieur LeBlanc's voice rose above the hum of the restaurant. "As you'll see on the schedule, our next stop is the famous Paris catacombs."

"What's a cat-comb?" demanded Bertie.

"The catacombs are sacred graveyards, but they are in tunnels deep underground," the guide told Bertie. He turned to Mr. and Mrs. Vanderhoff. "It's a remarkable place, but it may be frightening for a young child. If you'd like, I can find somewhere else—"

"I want to go!" Bertie interrupted. "I'm not scared."

"Of course my boy isn't scared," snapped Mr. Vanderhoff. "But what's so special about these old tunnels?"

"The rocks are fascinating," said William.

"Even more important, the catacombs are part of Paris's history," Frederick said enthusiastically. "The bones and skulls of thousands of people are buried there."

Bones and skulls! thought Samantha. Suddenly she felt queasy again.

Mrs. Gray looked worried, too. "I'd better tell Martha to take Prince back to the hotel," she said hesitantly. She looked around at the group. "But if everyone else wants to go to an underground graveyard, I guess I'll go with you."

"Very good," said Monsieur LeBlanc. He checked his watch. "You may all enjoy the view a bit longer. Then we'll travel to the catacombs." He smiled. "A guide there will lead us underground to the land of the dead."

chapter 5
A Dark Path

WHEN THEY ARRIVED at the catacombs, a man with sharp features and narrow brown eyes was smoking a cigarette in the entryway. In accented English, he introduced himself as Jacques, their guide to the tunnels. He warned them of steep stairs ahead and a dark, uneven path underground.

Grandmary decided to stay aboveground. Mrs. Vanderhoff declared that she'd keep Grandmary company. "I must be careful of my health," Mrs. Vanderhoff said, fanning her face. "I have terrible nerves."

Monsieur LeBlanc told Grandmary and Mrs. Vanderhoff that the tunnel's exit was near an historic church. "The omnibus will take you to the church, ladies, and we'll join you there in an hour or so."

As Grandmary and Mrs. Vanderhoff returned to the omnibus, Nellie whispered to Samantha, "The underground tunnels sound scary."

"We'll stay close together," said Samantha, trying to sound braver than she felt. "And the Admiral will be there, too."

"Remember to follow the path," called Jacques as he gave each member of the group a candle. "These tunnels were dug centuries ago. No one knows where they all lead. If you leave the path, you could enter the wrong tunnel and be lost forever."

There was silence among the group, and Samantha felt a chill go up her spine. She couldn't imagine anything worse than being lost in a dark underground tunnel.

Bertie hummed to himself and swung his candle around, not seeming to realize how serious the guide's words were. But his father spoke to him sharply. "You stay right beside me the whole time, Bertie," Mr. Vanderhoff ordered. "And Ingrid, you watch Bertie, too."

"Yes, sir," said Ingrid.

Jacques lit each of their candles in turn. "Other visitors may pass through, but be careful to stay with our group," he cautioned. "Along the path, there is a dark line on the ceiling. If you become lost, look for that line—it will lead you to the exit. And if an area is roped off, it is closed to visitors. Do *not*, under any circumstances, go there."

He stubbed out his cigarette. "Everyone is ready?" he asked, his eyes narrowing even further as he studied their faces. "Very well, let's begin."

Jacques led the way down steep stairs. Mr. Vanderhoff, Bertie, and Ingrid followed him. Then, with a nervous titter, Mrs. Gray stepped into the darkness.

"You girls go next," the Admiral told Samantha and Nellie. "I'll be right behind you."

Samantha took a deep breath. Holding tight to the railing, she started down the stairs, with Nellie following closely. Entering the darkness, Samantha heard the Admiral talking with Frederick and William, who were behind him, and Monsieur LeBlanc, who was last in the group.

Soon it was so dark that Samantha could see only Nellie, who was just a step behind her. Shadows from their candles danced on the wall as they went deeper.

When they reached the bottom of the stairs, Jacques stopped the group in front of a plaque written in French. The candle in his hand flickered as he said, "We are now entering the Kingdom of the Dead."

Samantha felt her heart beating fast. It was pitch-black down here, and the narrow path was hemmed in by rocks dripping water. For a moment, she wanted to hurry back up the stairs. But she held tight to her candle and forced herself to listen to the guide.

Hot wax trickled onto her hand as Jacques told the group, "Along this path, you will see the bones of people who have died over the centuries. They were originally buried in cemeteries all over Paris. But when the cemeteries became too crowded, the bones were brought here."

The group continued single file, but Samantha and Nellie tried to stay close together. Samantha gasped as she saw a skull. Only inches away from her hand, the hollowed-out head rested on a pile of bones. Its empty eye sockets seemed to be staring straight at her.

She heard Mrs. Gray exclaim, "Oh dear! The bones are everywhere!"

Samantha raised her candle and saw that Mrs. Gray was right. On either side of the path, skulls and bones were carefully stacked from floor to ceiling. Samantha felt a wave of panic as she realized that countless skeletons surrounded her in the darkness.

She took a deep breath and felt the cold, damp air fill her lungs. Then she turned around and saw that Nellie's face was white with fear. *I have to be brave for Nellie's sake,* Samantha told herself, and she gave Nellie's hand a reassuring squeeze.

Ahead, Mr. Vanderhoff's voice boomed through the tunnels. "Wait till I tell everyone back in Buffalo about this!" he declared enthusiastically.

As they went forward, Samantha discovered that the passageway twisted and turned, and sometimes she and Nellie lost sight of the rest of the group. Occasionally there were gaps along the path, where arched openings as large as doorways opened into other black tunnels. Heavy ropes were slung across many of the openings to show that visitors were not allowed to enter.

Samantha paused by one roped-off entrance and peered into the darkness. The light from her candle barely penetrated the shadows. When Nellie came up behind her, Samantha whispered, "I wonder what it leads to."

"Let's not look," Nellie said quickly. "Remember how the guide said that if we got lost, we might never be found?"

"I remember," said Samantha with a shiver. For a terrible moment, she wondered if she might already have turned in the wrong direction. She held up her candle and looked for the thick dark line on the ceiling. It was right above her head.

We must be on the right path, she told herself. But she was glad when the Admiral caught up with them and they continued on together.

They passed a few rock archways that were not roped off and led only to closet-sized nooks off the main path. When Samantha stepped inside one nook, she felt as if she'd walked into a tiny private room. The light of her candle revealed an inscription in Latin on one wall.

Someone must have carved that long, long ago, she thought. She put her candle closer to the wall. *I wonder what it means.*

Samantha turned to ask the Admiral, but there was no one nearby. Suddenly, she felt terribly alone in the darkness. "Grandfather? Nellie?" she called.

"We're over here, Samantha," came the Admiral's reply. Samantha walked toward the sound of her grandfather's voice. She found herself on the main path again, just a few feet from where she'd entered the tiny room.

As they continued through the catacombs, Samantha started to forget her fear. She stopped to examine ancient inscriptions, and she listened closely when Jacques told them tales from the catacombs' history.

Slowly, the group became spread out along the path. Samantha could hear voices around her, and she realized that Mr. Vanderhoff, Bertie, and Ingrid were walking quickly. William and Frederick, however, seemed to be lingering behind, and William often stopped to comment on rocks.

Samantha heard other visitors in the catacombs, too, and she sometimes had to squeeze to one side to let shadowy figures pass by. Once, after she had paused to make room for several people, Samantha found herself separated from Nellie, the Admiral, and the rest of the group. She paused, listening for their footsteps.

As she waited, she heard a thud. Then a voice exclaimed, "Oh dear!"

"Is that you, Nellie?" Samantha called nervously.

Nellie appeared at her elbow. "No, I think it came from ahead of us."

Together, Samantha and Nellie plunged forward along the path. Around the next curve, they found Mrs. Gray struggling to rise to her feet. "Let me help you," offered Samantha, reaching out to her.

"Thank you," said Mrs. Gray. She took Samantha's hand and rose unsteadily. Then she brushed off her long skirt. "Someone went past me. I moved to one side, and then I tripped over a rock."

"I almost tripped once, too," Nellie told Mrs. Gray. "Luckily, the Admiral was there."

Samantha glanced back, but the path behind her was dark. "Where *is* the Admiral?" she asked.

"He was behind me a few minutes ago," Nellie replied, looking around.

"He must be close by," Mrs. Gray assured them.

"Grandfather?" Samantha called. She held up her candle, expecting him to call out or come around the corner at any moment. But instead of his cheery voice, there was just a rustling noise nearby.

"Admiral?" Nellie shouted.

There was still no answer. Samantha's stomach tightened with fear. But now she wasn't afraid for herself. "Let's look for him," she urged Nellie, and together they started retracing their steps back down the path.

Mrs. Gray caught up with them. "Wait a moment, girls," she said, lifting her candle toward the ceiling. Samantha saw the black stripe, and Mrs. Gray nodded.

"Good," said the widow, gathering her long skirt with her free hand. "This is the right path."

Hurrying back down the shadowy pathway, Samantha and Nellie kept calling for the Admiral. They hadn't gone far when they heard Monsieur LeBlanc shout, "I need help! The Admiral is hurt!"

The girls started running. Rounding a corner,

Samantha saw the Admiral lying on the ground, with Monsieur LeBlanc leaning over him.

Samantha rushed forward and knelt beside her grandfather. She saw blood flowing from a gash on his forehead. For a terrible moment, Samantha remembered an accident in a storm long ago, when the Admiral had injured his head and been knocked unconscious. But now, as she took his hand, she was relieved to feel his strong grasp.

"Are you all right?" asked Nellie, leaning close.

William and Frederick came running up, and Jacques appeared from the other direction. Jacques spoke quickly in French to Monsieur LeBlanc and then hurried off.

"What's wrong?" William demanded. Without waiting for an answer, he took off his coat and put it over the Admiral. "Fred, put a clean handkerchief over that cut on his forehead," he ordered. Frederick followed his cousin's instructions.

Mr. Vanderhoff, Bertie, Ingrid, and Mrs. Gray

joined them. As the path became crowded, the Admiral struggled to say something. Samantha and Nellie both leaned closer. Samantha heard, "Be careful," but she couldn't understand the rest.

"We will," Nellie told the Admiral in a low voice.

Suddenly, everyone seemed to be talking at once. "He's bleeding!" gasped Mrs. Gray as Frederick's white handkerchief turned red. The widow staggered backward and looked as if she was about to faint.

Mr. Vanderhoff steadied her. Then he produced a bottle of smelling salts from his pocket. "I carry these for my wife when she has nervous spells," he said, waving the smelling salts under Mrs. Gray's nose.

"Please stay calm," Monsieur LeBlanc directed the group. "Jacques has gone to get help."

A few minutes later, Jacques reappeared along with two large men. He and the men carefully lifted the Admiral onto a stretcher and started toward the exit.

Samantha picked up the Admiral's top hat and cane, and she and Nellie followed close to the

stretcher. William and Frederick walked beside
the stretcher, too, and the rest of their group followed behind.

By the time they neared the exit, the Admiral was
struggling to sit up. "What's going on?" he asked,
confused. "Where are my hat and cane?"

"Here they are," Samantha said, putting the
cane in his hand and his hat by his head. "Please,
just rest now."

Finally they climbed up the steps and out into
fresh air. Samantha saw her grandmother waiting
by the exit. Grandmary was twisting her gloves
in her hand, and her face was tight with worry.
Mrs. Vanderhoff stood beside Grandmary, clucking
anxiously.

Grandmary, Samantha, and Nellie stayed by the
Admiral's side as the men carried him to the curb.
A doctor and a carriage were waiting there, and
the doctor examined the Admiral's forehead. Then
Grandmary told the girls that the Admiral was going

to the hospital to be checked for injuries, and she was going with him.

Samantha and Nellie wanted to go along, too, but Grandmary explained that there was no room in the carriage—and the Admiral wanted as little fuss as possible.

"I've arranged for you girls to stay with the tour group, and Mrs. Vanderhoff kindly offered to help if you have any problems," Grandmary instructed them. "Doris will be at the hotel when you get back. I hope your grandfather and I will be back soon, too."

Grandmary gave each girl a brief kiss on the forehead and then stepped into the carriage, and the driver flicked the horses' reins. Samantha blinked back tears as she watched the carriage roll away. Nellie said quietly, "Samantha, I'm worried about the Admiral."

"I'm worried, too!" said Samantha. She shivered in the frosty wind. "What a terrible accident!"

"But maybe it *wasn't* an accident," said Nellie. She

lowered her voice even more. "Remember what the Admiral tried to tell us after he fell?"

Samantha hugged her arms around herself. "All I heard was 'Be careful.' I guess he didn't want us to fall, too."

Nellie looked around. The rest of the group had gathered across the street, and the girls were alone. "The Admiral said, 'Be careful of the tour,'" Nellie whispered. "I thought he was going to say more, but then the other people crowded around us."

"'Be careful of the tour'?" Samantha repeated slowly. She frowned. "What did he mean?"

"I'm not sure," said Nellie. She glanced over at the tour group. "But I think he was trying to warn us about something—or someone."

chapter 6

Clues Underground

THE BITTER WIND gusted as Samantha and
Nellie stood outside the catacombs, and Samantha
felt chilled all over. She remembered the red-haired
man's warning that the Admiral might be in great
danger because of the secret letter. Now the Admiral
had tried to warn Samantha and Nellie about something, too.

But Samantha realized that Nellie didn't yet know
about the Admiral's secret letter, and she wondered
whether she should tell her. Samantha looked around.
The other members of the group were still across the
street, clustered around a kiosk where souvenirs and
sweets were sold. No one was in earshot. *What should
I do?* Samantha worried.

"Nellie," she said finally, "if I tell you a secret,

will you promise not to tell anyone?"

"Of course!"

Samantha nodded. Then, as quickly as she could, she whispered to Nellie everything she had learned about the important letter that the Admiral had taken to the Russian Embassy.

"Why didn't you tell me last night?" Nellie asked, her blue eyes searching Samantha's face.

"I promised the Admiral I wouldn't tell anyone," Samantha explained. "But now he's hurt, and maybe it *wasn't* an accident. Maybe someone was trying to steal the secret letter."

"Maybe—" Nellie began.

Just then, a voice rang out from across the street. "My wallet—it's gone!"

Samantha whirled around. Mr. Vanderhoff was standing near the kiosk, frantically checking his pockets. Other members of the group were looking on with concern. Samantha and Nellie hurried across the street to join them.

Mrs. Vanderhoff hovered near her husband, fanning her face despite the cold. "Good heavens! It can't be gone!"

Monsieur LeBlanc stepped forward. "Monsieur Vanderhoff, when did you last see the wallet?"

"I—I can't remember," said Mr. Vanderhoff, patting his pockets. "I had it when I left the hotel this morning." He shot an angry look at Jacques. "Maybe someone picked my pocket in the catacombs."

"Monsieur, in all my years at the catacombs, nothing has ever been stolen from *anyone* I've guided," said Jacques with great dignity. "Perhaps you dropped it when you were assisting the Admiral. If you like, I'll take you back to search."

"Yes, Robert, go look for it!" Mrs. Vanderhoff urged her husband.

Monsieur LeBlanc said he would help with the search. Ingrid, Frederick, and William volunteered to go, too.

The thought of going back into those pitch-black tunnels made Samantha's stomach churn. The catacombs seemed even more forbidding now, since the Admiral's accident—and his warning to be careful of the tour.

But if we go back, maybe we can find clues to what happened to the Admiral, Samantha thought. She and Nellie looked at each other, and then Nellie nodded.

"We'll help look, too," Samantha told Mr. Vanderhoff.

Mrs. Gray frowned. "I'm not sure that's wise, girls. It would be safer for you to wait with Mrs. Vanderhoff, Bertie, and me."

"I'll be with the girls," Ingrid reassured Mrs. Gray. She adjusted her glasses. "And it would be good to have as many people as possible."

"I'm afraid—" began Mrs. Gray.

Mrs. Vanderhoff interrupted her. "The girls have been left in *my* care, Mrs. Gray, and I'm sure they'll be safe with Ingrid." She turned to Samantha and Nellie. "And *do* try to find that wallet. It has quite a bit of money in it."

Jacques led the search party back into the catacombs. He was followed by Mr. Vanderhoff, Ingrid, Nellie and Samantha, William, and Frederick. Monsieur LeBlanc was again at the end of the group. The searchers stayed close together, their candles throwing shadows on the walls.

Why did the Admiral say that we should be careful of the tour? Samantha wondered. *Was it the path itself that he was warning us about—or someone in the group?*

Samantha walked quickly, keeping her eyes on the path and looking for any possible clue. She was so focused that she almost hit her head on a low-hanging rock, but she ducked just in time.

Then, as she passed a roped-off tunnel, she felt the hairs on the back of her neck prickle. Was something lurking in the shadows? She forced herself to pause and peer over the rope. All she saw was darkness, and she hurried on.

She and Nellie were able to stay close together until a group of tourists passed them on the path. In the flickering candlelight, Samantha noticed that all the tourists were looking down at the path. She could hardly even glimpse their faces.

A thief could easily hide in the tunnels down here, Samantha thought with a shudder. *And it's so dark that you could walk right past people and never recognize them.*

At the next turn, Jacques stopped the group. "Here is where the Admiral fell."

Samantha lifted her candle and studied the spot. There were no bones along this part of the tunnel, and the path turned in an *S* shape. Samantha realized that the Admiral probably would not have been seen by anyone when he fell.

Mr. Vanderhoff peered at the rocky floor. "Look

for a brown leather wallet," he told them. "It has a *V* on it."

The group spread out and began searching. "The rocks right here are dry, not slippery at all," Nellie whispered to Samantha.

Samantha crouched and ran her hand over the ground. *Nellie's right. It's as dry as a bone,* she thought. Then she remembered all the bones along the tunnels. She quickly pulled back her hand and stood up.

"I don't see anything the Admiral would have tripped on," continued Nellie, still examining the ground. Then she looked upward. "Look at that, Samantha." She held her candle up to a low-hanging rock that jutted from the ceiling, near the tunnel wall. "Do you think the Admiral could have hit his head on it?"

Samantha lifted her candle toward the rock. "It's about the Admiral's height. I guess he *could* have hit his head if he'd been walking very close to the wall."

"He might've moved over to let someone pass,"

suggested Nellie. "Then when he started walking again, he banged his head on the rock."

"Maybe," Samantha said doubtfully. She kept looking along the path. A few yards away, she paused at a roped-off archway. *This is just the sort of place where someone could've been hiding,* she thought.

Her heart beating fast, Samantha raised her candle and peered over the rope. Beyond the archway, the tunnel stretched into darkness.

Nellie joined her at the rope. "I don't think anything could be back there—it's too far from where the Admiral fell," she said, raising her candle beside Samantha's.

"You're probably right," Samantha agreed.

She was about to turn away when Nellie said, "Wait, I see something." Nellie stepped over the rope and picked up a small white object almost hidden by a rock. "Oh," she said. "It's just a scrap of paper."

Mr. Vanderhoff came around the corner. "Let me look at it. Maybe it's from my wallet."

He grabbed the paper and examined it by the light of his candle. "Looks like an address, but I've never seen it before." He dropped the paper, and it fluttered to the ground.

When Mr. Vanderhoff was out of sight, Samantha picked up the scrap. The address penciled on it was *14, rue du Jardin*.

"Nellie!" she whispered urgently. "This is the paper the chocolate maker gave the Admiral yesterday. It's the address of the other candy store."

Nellie leaned closer to look. "I remember now. The Admiral put it in his pocket." She frowned. "Why was it lying there, off the path?"

"Maybe it dropped out of the Admiral's pocket when he fell, and then the wind blew it over there," Samantha suggested.

"But there's no wind down here, Samantha," Nellie said quietly. "So, either the Admiral dropped it behind the rope, or—"

"Or someone else did," Samantha whispered.

She looked again into the darkness behind the rope. "Nellie, what if a thief had been hiding back there? He could have attacked the Admiral and stolen his wallet. He might've dropped the paper in the tunnel as he ran away."

Nellie's candle flickered as she nodded slowly. "It's possible."

"We'll save this for the Admiral," said Samantha, tucking the paper into her pocket. "Maybe he'll know why it was there."

As the group kept searching, they found a few small, shiny papers that looked like wrappers for sweets. "Someone must've been hungry," said Ingrid, examining a wrapper. She sounded tired.

"Don't worry about trash! Just look for the wallet," Mr. Vanderhoff snapped.

Frederick spoke up. "I think we're all getting hungry," he said calmly. "Perhaps it's time to leave."

"Yes, we've looked everywhere. The wallet isn't here," William added.

Mr. Vanderhoff reluctantly agreed to give up the search, and Jacques led them back to the exit. When they reached the stairs, Samantha climbed up eagerly. The wind outside was colder than ever, but it felt good to breathe fresh air again.

Monsieur LeBlanc offered to take the group to the Fortifications, the massive stone wall surrounding Paris. But only William and Frederick wanted to go with him. The rest of the group returned to the hotel in the omnibus. As they rode, Mr. Vanderhoff fumed about his wallet. "A pickpocket must've stolen it," he declared.

"Oh, Robert, we were right about the thieves in this city," exclaimed Mrs. Vanderhoff. She clutched her pearls as if afraid that a thief would break into the carriage and rip them from her neck.

"You should report the crime to the Paris police!" Mrs. Gray urged Mr. Vanderhoff. "Perhaps gangs of thieves are working underground. It might take time, but you could help the police catch them."

"There's no point in *my* wasting time at a police station," Mr. Vanderhoff replied irritably. "And I *believe* my wallet was taken in the catacombs, but I don't know for sure."

Samantha sank back into her seat, thinking hard. She didn't know why Mr. Vanderhoff's wallet had disappeared. But she did know that the red-haired man had warned of danger.

What really happened in the catacombs? Samantha wondered. *Did the Admiral just fall—or did someone try to steal the secret letter from him?*

chapter 7
Footsteps in the Night

WHEN SAMANTHA AND Nellie returned
to their suite, Doris greeted them at the door. "Your
grandmother is here—" she began in her loud voice.

Before Doris could say more, Samantha and Nellie
rushed into the sitting room, where Grandmary had
her travel case open on a luggage stand.

"Hello, girls. I'm glad you're here," said Grandmary with a weary smile. "I wanted to talk with you
before I return to the hospital."

The girls began peppering her with questions.
"How is the Admiral?" "Where is he?" "Is he better?"

"Your grandfather is feeling much better," said
Grandmary, arranging items inside the travel case.

"Thank heavens!" said Samantha. She felt a
weight lifted from her heart. But as she perched on

86

the sofa, she noticed that Grandmary's eyes lacked their usual sparkle. "When's he coming back?"

Grandmary placed her silver brush in the case. "He wanted to leave the hospital immediately," she said. "But his head still hurts, and he has no memory of the accident. The doctors have convinced him to stay a day or so longer, and I shall stay with him."

"He doesn't remember the accident at all?" Samantha asked.

Grandmary shook her head. "He remembers walking through the catacombs. Then, the next thing he knew, he was being carried out on a stretcher. The doctors say it's not uncommon for people to forget how they fell. So perhaps we'll never know what happened."

Doris brought in a stack of ironed clothes. "Here are the things you asked for, ma'am," she said. "Is there anything else I can get for you?"

"No, thank you, Doris," said Grandmary.

"Very well, ma'am," said the maid. "Please give

Admiral Beemis my very best wishes, ma'am. And I'll be in my room, if you need me."

As soon as Doris left, Samantha said, "Something else happened at the catacombs, too, Grandmary."

She and Nellie explained that Mr. Vanderhoff had discovered that his wallet was missing, and they had returned to the catacombs to search for it. They told Grandmary how they had found a low-hanging rock where the Admiral might have hit his head, and also a piece of paper that had been in the Admiral's pocket.

Nellie said anxiously, "Mr. Vanderhoff thinks *his* wallet was stolen. And we worried that..." She paused.

"That the Admiral might have been robbed, too," Samantha finished.

"Oh dear!" said Grandmary. She sat down on the edge of the sofa, her back ramrod straight as always. "Well, I suppose I might as well tell you—when we reached the hospital, your grandfather's wallet wasn't in his jacket. I looked for it, but it's disappeared."

Samantha sucked in her breath. *Grandfather **was** robbed!*

"Grandmary," Samantha said in a low voice, "last night I heard the Admiral talking with a man from the British Embassy. Afterward, he told me about the secret letter he was carrying. Was that stolen, too?"

"No," said Grandmary firmly.

Thank heavens! thought Samantha.

"Your grandfather told me that the letter is safe," Grandmary added. "He said there's no need to worry about it. So I presume he's finished with his mission and has delivered the letter to the British ambassador."

Nellie sighed with relief. "That *is* good news. We thought the Admiral might have been attacked because of the secret letter."

"Now, girls, don't let your imaginations run away with you," said Grandmary. She stood up again. "It seems that a common pickpocket was lurking

in the catacombs, and both your grandfather and
Mr. Vanderhoff were his victims. Perhaps the scoun-
drel pushed your grandfather, and he hit his head
on the rock you saw."

Grandmary closed the lid of her traveling case.
"We were warned about the thieves in Paris," she
said with a sigh. "And I'm grateful that your grandfather wasn't injured more severely."

"May Nellie and I go with you and visit him?"
Samantha asked hopefully.

Grandmary shook her head. "I'm sorry. No
children are allowed to visit."

"Not even family?" Nellie looked stricken.

"I'm afraid not, but he should return soon," said
Grandmary. "And—"

Before she could finish, there was a knock at the
front door. A moment later, Doris announced, "The
porter is here for your luggage, ma'am."

"You girls will be staying here at the hotel with
Doris, and I've left the hospital's name and address

on the desk," said Grandmary as she put on her hat and coat. "Mrs. Vanderhoff said you may accompany her family on the tour tomorrow, which is very kind."

Grandmary quickly kissed both girls good-bye. "Listen to Doris and don't get into mischief," she reminded them. Then the door closed behind her.

After their grandmother left, Samantha and Nellie sat silently across from each other on the twin beds in their room. The crate of gifts was still open on the floor, and it reminded Samantha of the Admiral's kindness and generosity.

He's always doing things for other people, she thought, staring down at the crate. *I wish we could help him now.*

Suddenly Nellie said, "We forgot to tell Grandmary what the Admiral said after we found him."

"I suppose he was trying to warn us about the

pickpocket," Samantha said sadly.

"But the Admiral said, 'Be careful of the tour…'" Nellie recalled. "I still think he wanted to tell us about somebody *on* the tour."

Samantha thought for a moment. "Maybe he meant Jacques," she said. "He knows the catacombs better than any of us. Mr. Vanderhoff practically accused Jacques of being a pickpocket, too."

Nellie shook her head. "Jacques was at the front of our group. I don't see how he could've robbed the Admiral."

"You're right," said Samantha. "But who else could it have been?"

There was a loud jangle as the telephone rang in the sitting room. Samantha heard Doris shout, "Hello!"

After a few moments, Doris came to their room and told them that they'd been invited to dine with the Vanderhoffs at the hotel restaurant.

"You're to meet them in the lobby at seven

o'clock," the maid told Samantha and Nellie. "I'll make sure your clothes are ready."

Just before seven o'clock, Samantha and Nellie, wearing their best dresses, said good-bye to Doris. The maid handed Samantha a long, heavy iron key. It was attached to a ring labeled *401*.

"I might not hear you knock when you return," said Doris. "So use this key to let yourselves in. After you're inside, lock the door again and pull the bolt across. Then come and tell me that you've returned."

"Yes, Doris," Samantha and Nellie replied together, and Samantha put the key in her pocket.

Their crisply ironed skirts rustled as they walked to the elevator. When the elevator doors opened, the operator looked at them questioningly. Samantha couldn't remember how to say "lobby" in French, but Nellie came to the rescue.

"*Le restaurant,* s'il vous plaît," she told the operator. He nodded and closed the elevator cage.

On the third floor, more guests entered, including Mr. and Mrs. Vanderhoff, Bertie, and Ingrid. As they all rode down to the lobby together, Samantha saw that Mr. Vanderhoff was now wearing a formal black suit, Mrs. Vanderhoff was in an emerald-green gown and matching emerald necklace, and even Bertie was sporting a jacket and tie. Ingrid still had on the same white blouse and black skirt that she'd worn earlier in the day, but she had added a ribbon tie at her collar.

Although the elevator was crowded, Mrs. Vanderhoff loudly asked Samantha and Nellie about the Admiral. "How is he feeling? Is he still in the hospital?" she demanded.

Samantha didn't want to talk about her grandfather in front of strangers, and she tried to answer in as few words as possible. She was careful not to mention the Admiral's missing wallet, and she noticed that Nellie didn't bring it up either.

When the elevator arrived in the lobby, Samantha hopped off quickly so that she could avoid Mrs. Vanderhoff's questions. She was glad when they stepped into the hotel's restaurant, where the chandeliers glittered and a buzz of conversation filled the air. They had just sat down at a table set with flowered china and gleaming silverware when Mrs. Gray came into the dining room. The young widow was wearing a long-sleeved black velvet dress with a simple diamond brooch at her neck, and she looked around the dining room uncertainly.

"Robert, go invite Mrs. Gray to join us," Mrs. Vanderhoff told her husband. "We can't let her eat by herself."

Mr. Vanderhoff grumbled but obeyed, and a moment later, he returned to the table with Mrs. Gray. "How is the Admiral?" asked Mrs. Gray as she took a chair next to Samantha. "I do hope he's feeling better."

Samantha was telling her about the Admiral's stay at the hospital when Ingrid said, "Oh look—there's Frederick and William!"

Samantha saw Frederick and William surveying the room. Both wore plain black suits, but Frederick's jacket looked much too big for him. Ingrid smiled eagerly, her cheeks turning pink and her eyes shining behind her glasses.

"Ingrid, you mustn't encourage those young men," Mrs. Vanderhoff said sternly. But Frederick and William crossed the dining room and sat at a table next to the Vanderhoffs'.

A moment later, William stood up and walked over to Samantha and Nellie. "How is the Admiral?" he asked.

The girls gave him the same information they had given the others.

But William began firing questions. "What hospital is the Admiral staying in? Do the doctors know why he fell? Does he have other injuries?"

Samantha and Nellie answered as best they could, but Samantha felt relieved when the waiter interrupted, bringing them their first course, a creamy soup.

"That young man *is* inquisitive, isn't he?" murmured Mrs. Gray as William returned to his table.

Privately, Samantha agreed. It seemed to her that Frederick and William were always asking about the Admiral. *Why are they so curious?* she wondered.

Waiters served the main course, beef topped with a rich sauce. Samantha was savoring the sauce when Monsieur LeBlanc came into the dining room. He headed straight for their table and asked about the Admiral. The girls gave their report, and Monsieur LeBlanc looked relieved. "I'm glad he's recovering."

Then Monsieur LeBlanc told everyone that he'd purchased the opera tickets that members of the group had requested. "But first, I would like to present each family with this souvenir from today."

With a flourish, he handed out several embossed

cardboard folders. Nellie and Samantha opened their folder and found a large black-and-white group photograph. It was the picture Monsieur LeBlanc had taken that morning at the Eiffel Tower.

Samantha and Nellie studied the photograph together. Mr. Vanderhoff had blinked, and Mrs. Gray was half-hidden by Ingrid, but everyone looked happy. Samantha felt a pang as she saw Grandmary and the Admiral sitting together, smiling.

I wish they could be here right now! she thought.

Next, Monsieur LeBlanc handed a ticket for an Italian opera to Mrs. Gray, and two tickets for a French opera to William and Frederick. Then he produced two more tickets for the French opera. "These are for you," he told Mr. Vanderhoff, but the mill owner waved him away.

"I've changed my mind. I won't be needing the tickets," said Mr. Vanderhoff, his mouth full of beef.

"But, monsieur, I've already purchased them," protested Monsieur LeBlanc. "You asked for the best seats, and they were quite costly."

Mr. Vanderhoff swallowed his beef. "I'm sure you understand that we've had a very difficult day, Monsieur LeBlanc, what with my wallet being stolen during *your* tour. I certainly don't expect to have to pay for those tickets." He leaned back in his chair. "My wife and I are tired, and we're going to sleep early. Perhaps we'll go to the opera tomorrow night instead."

Poor Monsieur LeBlanc! Samantha thought as the tour guide reluctantly put the tickets back into his pocket.

There was an awkward silence. Then Mrs. Gray asked, "Monsieur LeBlanc, can you tell me what time I can expect to return from the opera this evening?"

"Usually quite late, madame, probably after midnight."

"That *is* quite late," said Mrs. Gray. "I'll have to tell Martha not to wait up for me." With a look of concern, she turned to Samantha and Nellie. "I'm sorry your grandmother couldn't join us for dinner. Will she be back soon?"

"No, ma'am," said Nellie. "She's spending the night at the hospital with our grandfather."

"It's such a shame about your poor grandfather's accident. And my dear husband's wallet missing, too!" said Mrs. Vanderhoff. She patted her mouth with a napkin. "Well, I did try to warn everyone about the dangers of Paris."

"Yes," said Mrs. Gray, putting a protective hand on the diamond brooch she was wearing. "And I'm very glad you did."

Monsieur LeBlanc reminded everyone to be in the lobby at nine o'clock the next morning for the day's tour activities. "We have a busy day planned, and I hope to see you all there," he said with a pointed glance at the Vanderhoffs.

When Samantha and Nellie returned to their hotel suite, it took them a few tries to open the lock with the iron key. But finally they got the key to turn, and once they were inside, they locked the door again. Then Samantha pulled the bolt across, while Nellie went to Doris's room. "We're back," Nellie called.

There was no answer. Nellie knocked hard and tried again. "WE'RE BACK!" she shouted, but the effort brought on a fit of coughing.

"All right, all right, I hear you!" Doris replied. "Take your baths and go to sleep now."

The girls went to their bedroom, and Samantha put the photograph from the Eiffel Tower inside the tall wooden wardrobe that she and Nellie shared. *Grandmary and the Admiral will want to look at the picture later,* she thought.

Nellie started coughing again. "Do you want to take your bath first?" Samantha asked her.

Nellie paused to catch her breath before answering. "No, you go ahead," she said finally.

In the bathroom, Samantha filled the white

bathtub. As she soaked in the soothing water, she
tried to forget her worries.

The Admiral is going to be fine, she told herself.
*It was a pickpocket who stole his wallet, and it had nothing
to do with the secret letter. I was just imagining things.*

When she finally got out of the tub, the suite was
dark except for a sliver of light from the bedroom
that she and Nellie shared. "Sorry I was so long!" she
called to Nellie as she opened the door.

But Nellie wasn't there, and the heavy door key,
which Samantha had left on her bedside table,
was gone. There was a penciled note on her pillow:
Back soon.

Something must be wrong, Samantha thought.
She sat down on her bed, the damp ends of her hair
dripping on the blue coverlet. She was wondering
whether to search for Nellie when she heard the main
door open. A moment later, Nellie came into their
room, looking very serious.

"Nellie, I was worried about you!"

"I'm sorry, Samantha. I just went to the reading room. I thought I might find a book there," Nellie said. She reached into the wardrobe and pulled out her own bathrobe. "I'll go take my bath now."

Samantha noticed that her sister hadn't brought any books back with her. And it wasn't like Nellie to mysteriously go off on her own. Samantha said, "Nellie, if something were bothering me, I'd tell you."

Nellie was facing the wardrobe. "You didn't tell me about the Admiral's letter."

"The Admiral said not to tell anyone," Samantha reminded her. "But I did tell you today, after he got hurt." She paused. "Won't you tell me what's wrong?"

"Promise to keep it a secret?" Nellie turned around, and her eyes searched Samantha's.

"I promise." Samantha drew an imaginary X across her chest. "Cross my heart."

Nellie bit her lip for a moment. Then she burst out, as if she could no longer bear to keep the secret, "I keep coughing, Samantha—I can't help it.

I don't feel sick, but what if I am?"

Nellie's face was tight with fear. "I went to the reading room to see if they had books about what to do if you're sick," she continued. "When I was little, my mother had a book called *Mrs. Connally's Cures.* It had recipes for medicines. But I couldn't find anything like that in the reading room."

Samantha remembered how Nellie's parents had suffered coughs and fevers before they died. She also knew that many people in Nellie's old neighborhood had died of tuberculosis, a disease that often caused coughing.

Nellie must be so scared! Samantha thought. She jumped up. "Don't worry! Lots of people cough." Samantha made herself cough. "See? I just did it too."

"Samantha, you don't need to pretend!" said Nellie, laughing despite herself. Then she became serious again. "But what if I really am sick? A doctor might decide that I should be in the hospital here, and then you'd all have to sail back to New York without me.

I might not see you or Bridget or Jenny ever again."

Tears came to Nellie's eyes. Samantha had never seen her look so afraid.

"Oh no!" said Samantha. "We'd never do that!" She reached out and hugged her sister. Then she looked Nellie straight in the face. "The Admiral is in the hospital now, but do you think we'd ever sail away without him?"

"No," Nellie admitted. She hesitated and then said slowly, "But Bridget, Jenny, and I have been left behind before."

Samantha knew it was true. After Nellie's parents had died, Nellie and her sisters had been abandoned by an uncle and left in an orphanage.

"But you're part of our family now, and we'll stick together always!" Samantha insisted. "Remember how you helped me at the Eiffel Tower today? Do you really think I'd ever leave you?"

Nellie shook her head.

"And neither would Grandmary or the Admiral,

or Aunt Cornelia or Uncle Gard," Samantha continued. "I promise!"

"I'd never leave you either—you're a wonderful
sister," said Nellie, and she gave Samantha a hug.
Then she took a deep breath. "I'd better go take a bath
now. The steam really does make my cough better."

While Nellie was in the tub, Samantha changed
into her nightgown and wrapped herself in her soft
comforter. She picked up her Sherlock Holmes book
and tried to read in bed. Soon, though, the words
started to blur on the page, and she fell asleep to the
pinging of sleet falling outside.

But later in the night she woke up. The room was
dark, and tiny pellets of ice were striking the window.
For a moment Samantha thought the sound had
awakened her.

Listening closely, she heard a soft swish, like the
sound of book pages being turned. It was coming
from the sitting room.

Nellie must be up reading, Samantha thought. She

was about to turn over when she heard Nellie's peaceful snoring.

Samantha sat upright. As her eyes became accustomed to the darkness, she saw Nellie asleep in the next bed. *If Nellie is here, who's in the sitting room?*

Samantha heard another rustle of paper. She sat frozen, listening. *Is it a mouse?*

In the distance, a church bell rang. Samantha counted the chimes. It was eleven o'clock, way past Doris's bedtime.

Then she heard a creaking noise. It sounded like careful footsteps. Samantha felt her blood turn as cold as the sleet outside. She slipped out of bed and shook Nellie's shoulder.

"Wake up!" she whispered.

chapter 8
Search for a Thief

"WHAT?" NELLIE MURMURED, still half asleep.

"I hear noises," Samantha whispered. "I think someone's out there."

Nellie was instantly awake. She got up and tiptoed to the bedroom door. It was open a crack, and she eased it closed. Then, with a heavy clunk, she bolted the bedroom door from within.

Samantha knew that Nellie, who had once lived in a dangerous neighborhood, had guarded against thieves before. Nellie stood by the door, listening intently. Samantha stood by her, so scared she could barely breathe. The floor in the sitting room creaked as if someone was hurrying across it.

"Do you hear that?" Samantha whispered.

Nellie nodded. She went over to the crate of gifts. Quietly, she reached in, picked up Uncle Gard's walking stick, and handed it to Samantha. Then she took Aunt Cornelia's parasol for herself, holding it as if it were a baseball bat.

Samantha gripped the walking stick as she and Nellie listened again. She heard a click that sounded like a door shutting. Samantha stood frozen for what seemed like forever. It was so quiet that she could hear the clock in the sitting room ticking.

Finally, Nellie called out sharply, "Who's there?"

There was no answer. Samantha's heart was thudding. "Should we go look?" she whispered. "Maybe it was only Doris." She reached up to unbolt the door.

"No!" whispered Nellie, grabbing her arm. "What if it *wasn't* Doris?"

Samantha realized that Nellie was right. "Doris?" Samantha called. There was still no answer. She tried again, louder. "DORIS?"

"DORIS, ARE YOU THERE?" Nellie shouted.

There was still no answer. The walking stick was now damp with sweat where Samantha was holding it tight.

After what seemed like an eternity of waiting, Nellie said, "Let's unlock the door and run to Doris's room. Ready?"

Samantha took a deep breath. "Yes."

Nellie unbolted the door, and together they ran headlong across the sitting room and down the hall to Doris's room. The maid's door was locked, and they pounded on it.

"Doris! Let us in! DORIS!"

"What is it? What's going on?" Doris called. A light went on in her room, and Doris came out, wrapped in a plaid bathrobe, her hair in pins.

When Samantha and Nellie told her what they'd heard, Doris grabbed the walking stick from Samantha. "Don't worry, girls," she declared. "If someone's sneaking around here, I'll find him. And he'll be sorry!"

Armed with the walking stick, Doris turned on the hall light and checked the front door. "It's not locked," said Doris, sounding worried.

Samantha clearly recalled that she'd locked and bolted the door when she and Nellie had returned from dinner. Then she remembered that Nellie had gone out again later. Nellie looked pale.

"I thought I'd locked it, but maybe I forgot," Nellie whispered.

Doris headed into the sitting room, the walking stick firmly gripped in her hand. As soon as she entered the room, she turned on all the lights. Then she looked behind the sofa and the armchairs. "No one's in this room," Doris said finally. She pointed to the telephone perched on the writing desk. "Samantha, call the hotel operator. Tell him we need help in Suite 401."

Samantha hurried to the telephone and picked up the receiver. She pressed down the switch, and an operator said something in French.

"We need help," said Samantha. Her voice sounded shaky even to her own ears. "Suite 401."

The operator answered in a flurry of words that Samantha couldn't understand. She was so nervous she struggled to remember even the French numbers. Staring down at the newspaper-covered desk, she said "4-0-1" in French. The operator repeated the numbers.

"Yes," said Samantha, glancing around to make sure the intruder hadn't suddenly appeared behind her. She was going to say more, but the operator clicked off. *I hope he understood,* she thought as she hurried to rejoin Doris and Nellie.

Doris was checking the other rooms, turning on every light. Nellie followed her, still holding the parasol, and Samantha kept close watch all around them.

Finally, they returned to the sitting room. "There's no one here," Doris announced, handing the walking stick back to Samantha. "And nothing seems to be missing. Your grandmother's jewelry is still on her dressing table."

Someone knocked loudly and called out "Hotel!" Doris opened the door. A sleepy-looking young woman with brown curls tucked into her maid's cap said, "Good evening, ma'am. The operator said you called, but he didn't know what you needed. He sent me because I speak English. May I help you?"

"No," Doris said. "We thought there was an intruder, but it seems we were wrong." She sighed wearily. "Maybe you could ask someone to bring us a tray of hot chocolate. We're all tired."

"I'm sorry, the hotel doesn't send food to rooms after ten o'clock," the maid said. She hesitated. "But if you'd like, I'll see if someone is still in the kitchen downstairs and could make you a tray."

Samantha felt her heart beat faster. *If there's no food sent up after ten o'clock, who came to our door late last night?* she wondered.

Doris shook her head. "No, don't bother them," she told the maid. "We'll be all right."

"Very good, ma'am. My name is Claire, and I'll

be cleaning rooms on this floor tomorrow. Please let me know if you need anything then."

"Thank you, Claire," Doris said. She locked and bolted the door, and then she turned to Samantha and Nellie. "Go back to bed, girls. You had a terrible day, what with the Admiral getting hurt and all. It's no wonder your imaginations ran away with you. And if I were you, Miss Samantha, I wouldn't read any more of those detective stories, either!"

As Doris began turning off the lights, Samantha and Nellie returned to their room. They tucked the walking stick and parasol back into the crate. Then Samantha threw herself on her bed. "I didn't imagine it! There *was* somebody in the sitting room." She wrapped herself in her comforter. "And I think someone tried to get in last night, too."

Samantha told Nellie how she had heard a knock on the door the previous night and someone had claimed to be bringing food. "But it was past eleven o'clock, and Claire said that no food is sent up after ten o'clock." Samantha shivered. "Maybe the person who sneaked in here tonight tried to come in last night, too."

"Should we tell Doris?" asked Nellie.

"I don't think she'd believe us," said Samantha. "And I don't understand why the thief broke in and then didn't steal anything—even Grandmary's jewelry."

"He might have been scared off when he realized we were awake," Nellie suggested.

"You're right!" Samantha said, sitting up straighter. "He probably only searched the sitting room. I'm sure I heard papers rustling, and the newspapers on the desk look messy now."

Nellie's eyebrows shot up. "The Admiral always leaves his newspaper folded. He likes everything 'shipshape.'"

"I'll show you what they're like now," said Samantha, throwing off her comforter. "Come on!"

Samantha led Nellie back into the shadowy sitting

room. Even though she knew the room had been thoroughly searched, she glanced around nervously. As soon as she reached the desk, she switched on the lamp. The London newspaper lay scattered under the light.

"I see what you mean," said Nellie. She picked up the newspaper and started folding it neatly. "But why would a thief go through old papers? It doesn't make sense."

Samantha was straightening the pages when a story caught her eye. "Nellie, look at this!" She pointed to a headline: *British Ambassador to Return to Paris Friday.*

She read aloud from the article. It said that the British ambassador had left Paris unexpectedly on Monday but was returning Friday and would host an event Friday evening. "Today is only Thursday," Samantha said, looking up from the paper. "So the ambassador hasn't come back to Paris yet."

"Why is that important?" asked Nellie, frowning.

"Because the Admiral said that he'd give the secret letter only to the ambassador—no one else," Samantha whispered. "But if the ambassador hasn't returned to Paris yet, then the Admiral *couldn't* have given him the letter today."

"But the Admiral told Grandmary the letter was safe," Nellie objected.

"Maybe he still has it—and he's hidden it somewhere safe," said Samantha, her mind whirling.

Nellie put back the folded newspaper, and Samantha switched off the light. Then the girls hurried back to their room. Once their door was locked, Samantha wrapped herself up in her comforter again. "Nellie, what if the person who knocked down the Admiral in the catacombs *was* trying to steal the letter? He took the Admiral's wallet, but he didn't find the letter there, so he came here tonight to search for it."

Nellie sat across from Samantha, her comforter wrapped around her like a cloak. "Only the people in our tour group knew that the Admiral was going to be in the catacombs today," said Nellie slowly.

"So the thief must be someone in our group!" Samantha finished for her. It was a frightening thought, and for a moment both girls sat frozen. Then Samantha went over to the wardrobe and took out the folder Monsieur LeBlanc had given them, along with a pencil and paper.

"Here's our picture from today," she said, sitting down next to Nellie and opening the folder. "I think the whole group was at the Eiffel Tower—I don't see anyone missing, do you?"

Nellie looked carefully. "Mrs. Gray's maid, Martha, was walking Prince, so she isn't in the picture," she noted. "And Monsieur LeBlanc took the photograph, so he isn't in it, either. But he was at the catacombs today, and he was here at the hotel tonight."

"Let's make a list of everyone," said Samantha. She jotted down names on the paper:

Mrs. Gray
Martha
Mr. Vanderhoff
Mrs. Vanderhoff
Ingrid
William Keller
Frederick Keller
Monsieur LeBlanc

Pointing to the first name on the list, Samantha said, "All we know about Mrs. Gray is that she's a widow and she hasn't traveled much before. But she seems nice."

"She seems scared of everything," Nellie said doubtfully. "Remember how she almost fainted in the catacombs? I don't think she's brave enough to be a thief." Nellie pointed at the next name. "Her maid, Martha, is grouchy, though—I don't even think she likes Prince."

"Yes, but Martha didn't come with us to the catacombs," Samantha reminded her.

"That's true," Nellie agreed. "And neither did Mrs. Vanderhoff."

Samantha tapped her pencil by the Vanderhoffs' names. "They are so rich—it's hard to imagine they would be thieves. Besides, Mr. Vanderhoff says his wallet was stolen in the catacombs, too—although I guess a pickpocket could've stolen it somewhere else."

The girls considered Ingrid next. They both had trouble picturing the cheerful young nanny as a thief, but they admitted that it was possible.

"She's not rich, and she speaks German," Samantha said slowly. "The Admiral said Germany and some other countries want to find out what's in the secret letter. Maybe Ingrid was hired to steal it."

"But even if her family used to be German, Ingrid is American now," Nellie pointed out. "Besides, Frederick and William speak German, too, and so does Monsieur LeBlanc."

Nellie hesitated. "But something strange *did* happen this evening," she continued. "When I was coming up from the reading room, I didn't want anyone to see me, so I used the stairs instead of the elevator. A woman in a coat and hat ran down the stairs as I was climbing up. I couldn't quite see her face, but I was almost sure it was Ingrid. I said hello, but she just hurried past me without saying anything."

"Let's ask her about it tomorrow," said Samantha. She drew a light question mark by Ingrid's name.

"I wonder about William and Frederick," Samantha continued. She was tired, and she rubbed her eyes as she forced herself to study the photograph one more time.

In the picture, both William and Frederick were looking straight ahead, and there was a strong resemblance between them. Samantha believed they were cousins. But she had a nagging suspicion that they were hiding something.

"When we were out with the Admiral yesterday, I kept seeing William and Frederick," she told Nellie. "It was almost as if they were watching us, and they've both been asking lots of questions about the Admiral."

"They both wanted everyone to go to the catacombs, too," Nellie said, fighting back a yawn. She pointed at the last name on the list. "We shouldn't forget about Monsieur LeBlanc, either. He seems to know everything about Paris, but we don't know much about him."

"I wish we knew more about *everyone* on the tour," said Samantha as she stifled a yawn. She could hardly keep her eyes open, and both girls decided it was time for bed.

Samantha stood up to put away the photograph. But as she took one last look at it, she saw her grandfather's face looking up at her.

Grandfather could still be in danger, she thought. *We have to find out who is trying to steal the letter.*

chapter 9

A Mysterious Caller

IN THE MORNING, sunlight was pouring through the white curtains in their room when Doris called, "Rise and shine!"

Doris told Samantha and Nellie that Mrs. Gray had just telephoned. "She asked if you would stop by her suite, number 404. If you get dressed and go now, your breakfast should be here by the time you get back."

Samantha and Nellie quickly brushed their teeth and got dressed, and then they headed down the hall in the opposite direction from the elevator. It was still early. The corridor was empty, except for shoes that had been left out the previous night for the hotel's free shoeshine service. Pairs of shoes were now polished and waiting by the guests' doors.

123

Nellie knocked at 404, and Martha opened the door wearing a pressed maid's uniform. Prince, who was dressed in a red plaid jacket and matching bow, darted around Martha, barking enthusiastically.

"Hello, Prince," said Samantha, patting his silky head. "Don't you look handsome!"

Mrs. Gray stepped into the entry hall and picked up the dog. "Thank you for coming, girls," she welcomed them. "I'm sorry Prince barked at you. He's usually a very good boy, but he *does* like to bark." She looked down at her dog fondly. "But you never bark at Mummy or Martha, do you, Prince?"

Smiling, Mrs. Gray invited the girls inside and led them to her sitting room. It was decorated in light blue instead of yellow but otherwise looked almost identical to the sitting room in 401. Samantha and Nellie sat together on the sofa while Mrs. Gray settled in an armchair and held Prince on her lap.

"Last night, something rather peculiar happened to me," said Mrs. Gray, and her eyes looked troubled.

"Afterward, I noticed that there was a light on in your suite. I wondered if by any chance you might have seen or heard anything unusual."

Samantha exchanged a glance with Nellie and then said cautiously, "We thought we heard someone in our suite, but we didn't find anyone. Nothing seemed to be stolen, either."

"The very same thing happened to me!" Mrs. Gray exclaimed. She told them that she'd become tired at the opera and decided to leave after the first act. When she'd arrived back at her suite, Martha had already gone to bed.

"I'd just gone to bed myself, when I heard someone in the sitting room," said Mrs. Gray. "I thought it must be Martha, and I called to her, but there was no answer. So I got up, and I was about to go into the sitting room when..." She paused.

"What happened?" Samantha asked.

"Well, I believe I heard the front door close. But when I checked the suite, nothing seemed out of place. Martha's door was closed, and I didn't want to wake her. At first, I thought that I was just being silly. But now I believe that someone came into my suite— he must have left when he heard me call Martha!"

Samantha and Nellie looked at each other. "Do you think it was a thief?" asked Nellie, sitting forward in her chair.

"I don't know what to think," said Mrs. Gray. She stroked Prince thoughtfully. "It's very odd, isn't it? I wondered if I should report it to the hotel." She hesitated. "But I'm afraid it may have been partly my own fault, since I forgot to lock the door when I came in. How foolish of me!" She gave a little laugh.

Martha had stepped into the sitting room, and now she cleared her throat discreetly. "If you'll excuse me, ma'am, perhaps it was just another hotel guest who opened the wrong door by mistake. All the doors look alike. And it doesn't appear that anything was stolen..."

"You're right, Martha," said Mrs. Gray. She looked

relieved. "But from now on, I'll keep my valuables in the hotel safe. You girls should advise your grandparents to do so, too. And if you need any help, please don't hesitate to call on me." She smiled cheerfully. "Stop by whenever you like."

Samantha and Nellie thanked her. They were about to leave when Nellie asked what time it was when Mrs. Gray heard the intruder. "I believe it was just past eleven," Mrs. Gray said.

Just after we heard the noises in 401, Samantha thought.

When Samantha and Nellie returned to their suite, a silver breakfast tray was waiting on the dining table. "Sit down and eat," Doris said, pouring them cups of hot chocolate. "It'll soon be time for you to go on the tour."

After Doris went back to her own room, Nellie said, "Well, I guess Mrs. Gray isn't the thief. The intruder came to her room last night, too."

Samantha nodded. She thought back to the conversation with Mrs. Gray and Martha. "Nellie, do you think it's possible that the person we heard in our suite was just a hotel guest who got confused?"

Nellie pulled apart a flaky croissant before she said, "No, I don't think so. If the person had thought he was in his own hotel room, wouldn't he have turned on the light? And why be so quiet?"

"You're right," said Samantha, buttering the croissant on her own plate. "But, Nellie, if the thief was looking for the Admiral's letter, why did he go into Mrs. Gray's suite?"

"Maybe after he ran out of our suite, he heard someone coming and looked for somewhere to hide," Nellie suggested. "Mrs. Gray said her door was unlocked."

Samantha put down her butter knife with a clink. "I've been wondering why the thief searched our suite last night," she said thoughtfully. "We know the Admiral took the letter to the Russian Embassy yesterday morning, and I thought he went straight to the Eiffel Tower afterward. But what if he came back *here* first instead? He might have hidden the letter somewhere in the suite."

Nellie stood up. "Doris would know if he'd been here. Let's ask her."

Samantha and Nellie found Doris ironing clothes in her tiny bedroom off the entry hall. "The hotel charges outrageous prices to do laundry, so I'm doing it myself," Doris announced in her loud voice. "Samantha, you got chocolate on your dress yesterday—please be more careful. And don't you girls put your shoes out in the hall like other people in this hotel do," she added. "I don't trust the hotel to take care of 'em properly—*I'll* polish them myself."

"Yes, Doris," Samantha and Nellie said together. Then Samantha asked, "Did the Admiral come back here yesterday after his meeting, before he went to join us on the tour?"

Doris nodded. "He was here late in the morning. He dropped off his briefcase."

"Of course!" said Samantha, remembering that the Admiral had left the hotel with his briefcase but hadn't been carrying it at the Eiffel Tower.

He must have left the secret letter inside it! Samantha thought. "Do you know where the briefcase is?" she asked Doris.

"In the Admiral's wardrobe," Doris said, frowning. "Why are you so curious?"

But Samantha and Nellie were already hurrying to their grandparents' bedroom, a sunny room with a large four-poster bed, two armchairs, a marble dressing table, and a pair of tall wooden wardrobes. Grandmary's dresses filled the first wardrobe, but the girls found the Admiral's suits and ties hanging in the second wardrobe. They looked behind the suits and discovered the leather briefcase.

Samantha and Nellie quickly unbuckled the briefcase and opened it. Inside, they found a square box

tied with a gold ribbon. Samantha pulled out the box
and untied the ribbon.

"Fancy chocolates!" she exclaimed after she
opened the lid. Never had she felt so disappointed to
see candy. There was a small card inscribed, *For my
beloved Mary.*

Nellie put the top back on the box. "I guess the
Admiral finally found the chocolates he wanted to
give Grandmary," she said as she retied the ribbon.
"He probably hid them here because he wanted to
surprise her."

Samantha checked through the side pockets of
the briefcase. All she found were two pencils and
a clean handkerchief.

"If the Admiral didn't put the secret letter in
his briefcase or his wallet, he could have hidden it
anywhere," said Samantha with a sigh. She eyed the
heavy furniture in the room, the clothes hanging in
the wardrobe, and long curtains on the windows.
"I don't know where we should look next."

"Neither do I," said Nellie sadly. She was tucking the briefcase back into the wardrobe when Doris appeared in the doorway.

"What are you girls doing in your grandparents' room?" she asked. She shooed them out and told them that it was time to get ready for the tour.

Samantha and Nellie put on their coats and mittens. Then, before they left, they reminded Doris not to let anyone into the suite while they were gone.

"As if I would!" said Doris, annoyed. "Now off you go!"

As the girls headed down the hall to the elevator, Samantha had an idea. "Nellie, remember how Mrs. Gray said our grandparents should keep their valuables in the hotel safe?"

"I remember."

"Well, maybe that's where the Admiral put the secret letter."

Nellie nodded with determination. "Let's find out."

In the lobby, they headed straight for the hotel

manager's desk. Monsieur Andreyev greeted them with a smile. "Good morning, young ladies. I hope your grandfather is feeling better."

"Yes, thank you, sir," said Samantha. Then she asked him if, by any chance, the Admiral had put any papers in the hotel safe.

Monsieur Andreyev passed a hand thoughtfully over his luxurious mustache. "Usually, I don't give out that sort of information—but, well, under these circumstances, let me see." He called an elderly man over and said, "Monsieur Dupont, these girls would like to know if their grandfather, Admiral Beemis, left any papers in our safe."

Monsieur Dupont began to answer in French, but Monsieur Andreyev said, "English, please."

Monsieur Dupont turned to Samantha and Nellie. "No," he said slowly. "Your grandmother called on the telephone yesterday. I told her there was nothing."

"Our grandmother called you?" echoed Samantha.

The old man nodded. "*Oui.* Madame Beemis, yes?

She was upset about your grandfather's accident."

"Yes," said Samantha slowly. She started to turn away, but Nellie asked shyly, "Excuse me, sir. What time did our grandmother call?"

The old man shrugged. "About five o'clock. I was just about to leave."

Monsieur Andreyev frowned. "Is there some problem I can help with, girls?"

"No, monsieur," said Samantha quickly. She and Nellie thanked him and then headed into the lobby. It was ten minutes before nine, and no one else from the tour group had arrived yet.

Samantha sat on the edge of an armchair. "At five o'clock, Grandmary was taking the Admiral to the hospital. She certainly wasn't telephoning the hotel. Who could have made that call?"

"It has to be someone from our tour group," Nellie said in a low voice. "Who else would have known that the Admiral had been hurt—and that we are staying at this hotel?"

"Whoever pretended to be Grandmary must have been looking for the secret letter," Samantha said slowly. "So the caller was probably the person who came into our room last night."

Samantha thought back to their list of suspects. They'd crossed off Mr. and Mrs. Vanderhoff and Mrs. Gray—but Ingrid, Frederick, and William were still on the list. And maybe Martha and Monsieur LeBlanc. *One of them must have made the call!* she thought.

"Nellie, do you think it really was a woman who called the hotel desk, or could a man have pretended to be Grandmary?"

"I'm not sure," said Nellie. "But—"

"Good morning, girls!" Monsieur LeBlanc's voice came from across the lobby. "Are you ready for the tour today? It will be very exciting!"

Samantha and Nellie exchanged a glance. "We're ready," said Samantha.

chapter 10

The Telltale Shoes

AS SAMANTHA AND Nellie waited for the rest of the group to arrive, Samantha decided that she would keep a close eye on all the tour group members. *I'll be a detective,* she told herself. *And I'll look for clues everywhere.*

Mrs. Gray was the first to join them in the lobby. As usual, she was fashionably dressed from head to toe. Her black coat was trimmed with fur, and her hat was topped with a froth of feathers in the latest style. Even her dainty boots were polished to a shine.

Sherlock Holmes might see something important about Mrs. Gray, but I don't, thought Samantha.

The young widow greeted the girls warmly.

"Is Prince coming on the tour today?" Nellie asked hopefully.

"No, he's staying here with Martha this morning. Monsieur LeBlanc said we're going to Notre-Dame Cathedral. I don't believe the church would welcome a dog—even one as well-behaved as Prince."

"I wish Prince was here!" said Bertie, racing up to them. He was followed by Ingrid and Mr. and Mrs. Vanderhoff. Samantha didn't see anything unusual about Mr. or Mrs. Vanderhoff, but she noticed that Bertie had a bit of jam around his mouth.

It must be left over from breakfast, she thought. *But it doesn't take a detective to notice that.* Then she realized that usually a nanny would make sure a child's face was clean. But Ingrid hadn't wiped off Bertie's jam stain.

Samantha studied Ingrid more closely. The nanny was wearing the same black skirt, white blouse, and brown wool coat that she had worn yesterday. Her blonde hair was pinned up neatly—but her lace-up shoes were mud-stained.

That's odd! thought Samantha. She wondered why

Ingrid hadn't put her shoes out to be cleaned and shined the previous evening. She remembered that Nellie had seen a woman that she thought was Ingrid on the hotel stairway last night.

Samantha didn't want to suspect the cheerful nanny, but she felt a jolt of worry when she looked at Ingrid's muddy shoes. The Vanderhoffs had said they were going to sleep early. Where had Ingrid gone? And had she returned too late to put her shoes out?

Frederick arrived a few minutes after nine o'clock. "My cousin will be joining us later," he told Monsieur LeBlanc. "He has, um, an errand to do this morning."

What errand would keep William away from the tour? wondered Samantha. Watching Frederick, Samantha noticed that he hadn't yet put on his hat, and his hair looked untidy. He seemed nervous as he quickly clamped his hat onto his head. She exchanged a glance with Nellie, who nodded slightly.

"Let's begin!" Monsieur LeBlanc announced to the

group. "Today we shall explore the Louvre, one of the world's greatest museums, and visit the magnificent Notre-Dame Cathedral." He smiled mysteriously. "Then, after lunch, I hope to have a surprise for you— but it will depend on the weather."

I hope we're not going up into the Eiffel Tower again, thought Samantha, remembering how dizzying the height was. But she didn't have time to ask Monsieur LeBlanc because the group was starting through the lobby. Nellie grabbed her arm. "We have to catch up with Ingrid," she whispered.

Walking fast, the girls maneuvered themselves next to Ingrid, who was at the back of the group. Samantha heard Nellie say casually, "I saw you on the stairs last night, Ingrid. I said hello, but I don't think you saw me."

"You couldn't have seen me," Ingrid replied, blushing bright red. "I didn't go anywhere last night." Then she hurried after Bertie, who was running ahead.

Doubt gnawed at Samantha as Ingrid rushed away. She was almost sure that the nanny was not telling the truth.

Outside it was clear and cold, and the sun glittered on frozen puddles. As the omnibus took them to the Louvre, Samantha and Nellie sat near Ingrid, and they shared a carriage blanket with her. But Samantha noticed that the nanny never once talked to them or looked in their direction.

When they arrived at the Louvre, Ingrid continued to avoid Samantha and Nellie. The museum was crowded with tourists speaking many different languages. It was hard for Samantha and Nellie to speak privately, but they finally found a quiet corner in a gallery filled with statues. Keeping their voices low, the girls agreed that Ingrid was acting strangely. "If she didn't do anything wrong, there's no reason for her to be avoiding us today," said Samantha.

"She could be afraid of getting into trouble," suggested Nellie. "The Vanderhoffs probably don't allow her to go out in the evening. Maybe she's worried that she'd lose her job if they found out."

"That could be," said Samantha. She looked around and saw Ingrid and Frederick talking together in the next gallery. Bertie was running through the gallery, darting among the statues.

Ingrid glanced over at Samantha and Nellie. Then she quickly looked away again. "Come along, Bertie!" she called.

"I'm sure Ingrid is hiding something," Samantha whispered to Nellie.

"Bertie," Ingrid called again. "We'd better go."

Bertie darted off, zigzagging around the statues as if they were an obstacle course, and Ingrid followed after him.

As the group left the gallery, Samantha and Nellie looked for a chance to talk to Ingrid, but Frederick stayed beside the nanny, helping her entertain Bertie.

"I think Frederick likes Ingrid," whispered Nellie

as Monsieur LeBlanc showed them famous paintings in another gallery.

"I think so, too," Samantha whispered back. "I hope he doesn't find out that she's really a thief." Samantha glanced at the crowds of visitors admiring the paintings. "I wonder, why did William decide to go on an errand instead of coming here?"

"Yes, that *is* strange," whispered Nellie. "But it's possible he doesn't like museums."

Or maybe he's the thief, and he's searching for the Admiral's letter, Samantha thought uneasily.

chapter 11

Whispers in the Cathedral

AFTER VISITING THE museum, the group returned to the omnibus. Ingrid took a seat as far away from Samantha and Nellie as possible.

Ingrid used to be so friendly, thought Samantha. *Why is she avoiding us now?*

The horses' hooves clip-clopped as they followed a stone-paved boulevard along the River Seine. The omnibus stopped just before a wide, arched bridge. "We'll get out and walk across," said Monsieur LeBlanc.

As the freezing wind blew white clouds across the blue sky, Monsieur LeBlanc led the group across the bridge to an island in the middle of the river. He stopped in front of an enormous stone church, and the tour group clustered around him.

"This island is the ancient center of Paris," Monsieur LeBlanc told them. "And here is Notre-Dame Cathedral, one of the greatest cathedrals in the world."

"Jeepers!" murmured Samantha, staring upward. She'd seen large churches before, but this immense structure was as big as a castle. At the cathedral's base, massive arches soared several stories high. Above the arches, Samantha saw spectacular stained-glass windows and carved stone balconies. High above the windows, enormous stone towers rose to the sky.

"What are those things up there?" asked Bertie, pointing to fierce-looking stone figures crouched near the roofline.

"Those are gargoyles," said Monsieur LeBlanc. "They're statues that catch rain coming from the roofs." He smiled. "They're also supposed to scare away evil spirits."

As Monsieur LeBlanc described how the cathedral had been built centuries ago, the bitter wind blew harder. Nellie started to cough. Mrs. Gray leaned toward her and asked, "Are you all right, dear?"

"Yes," Nellie gasped, and then she coughed again. "I think it's the wind," she said, turning away from the group and covering her face with her handkerchief.

Monsieur LeBlanc was telling stories and didn't see Nellie doubled over with coughing. Samantha decided it was time to take action. "Let's go inside," she whispered.

Guiding Nellie by the elbow, Samantha led her through the cathedral's doors. As they stepped inside the cavernous space, Samantha smelled incense and candles burning, and she heard an organ playing softly. The huge cathedral was full of visitors, but everyone was speaking in hushed tones.

When Nellie stopped coughing, she took a deep breath. "Oh, Samantha!" she said, gazing up at the soaring ceiling. "It's beautiful! And look at the stained glass—"

"Where's everyone else?" a man's voice broke in.

Samantha turned and saw William behind them. He looked serious, as usual, and his question echoed in the silence of the church.

"They're coming in now," said Samantha, glancing at the doors. Monsieur LeBlanc was gesturing toward the vaulted ceiling as he led Mrs. Gray, Mr. and Mrs. Vanderhoff, Bertie, Ingrid, and Frederick inside.

William nodded and then turned back to Samantha and Nellie. "I visited Admiral Beemis at the hospital this morning," he said abruptly.

For a moment, Samantha was speechless. Why had William visited the hospital? She stammered, "How-how is the Admiral?"

"He appears better, but he still doesn't remember how he fell." William frowned. "Do you girls have any idea?"

Samantha was about to reply, but Nellie spoke up. "No," she said firmly.

"Well, your grandfather should be back at the

hotel soon—probably tonight," William replied. Then he headed toward the tour group.

"Why on earth did he go see the Admiral?" Nellie whispered.

"I don't know, but I'm afraid," Samantha whispered back. "What if William went to the hospital to look for the letter?"

Mrs. Vanderhoff tapped on Samantha's shoulder. "Stay with the group," she instructed sharply.

Nellie and Samantha rejoined Monsieur LeBlanc as he was quietly telling everyone about the huge towers. "You may climb one of the towers if you wish," he offered. "It's about four hundred steps in all, and it may be cold up there, but you can see the gargoyles face-to-face."

William was the first to say that he'd like to climb the tower. Then Frederick and Ingrid raised their hands, too.

But Bertie tugged Ingrid's arm. "I don't want to go!" he declared.

"It'll be fun, Bertie," Ingrid said in a low voice. "You'll get to see the gargoyles."

"I don't want to see them," Bertie protested.

"You don't have to go, Bertie," Mrs. Vanderhoff interjected. "Ingrid will stay with you in the cathedral. Won't you, Ingrid?"

Ingrid blushed. "Yes, ma'am."

As William and Frederick headed away from the group, Samantha whispered, "Nellie, why don't you watch Ingrid? I'll follow William and Frederick."

Nellie nodded. "All right. But be careful, Samantha!"

Samantha told Monsieur LeBlanc that she had decided to climb the tower, too.

"If you hurry, you can catch up with the Canadian gentlemen," Monsieur LeBlanc advised her.

Following signs to the tower, Samantha walked quickly through the church until she was out of Monsieur LeBlanc's view. Then she slowed down. She didn't want to catch up with William and Frederick.

She just wanted to keep an eye on them.

The tower entrance was outside the cathedral, and several visitors were waiting to climb the steps. Samantha saw that William and Frederick, both holding their hats in the stiff wind, were next to last in the line, directly in front of a French family with several children. Samantha slipped into the line behind the French children while the Canadians were absorbed in conversation. She was almost sure William and Frederick hadn't seen her, and she slunk down to make herself even less visible.

As the line moved forward, Samantha listened for snatches of English. She heard Frederick say, "You should have told the truth from the beginning, Will."

"I'm not the only one who's been keeping secrets," William shot back. "What about you?"

Her heart pounding, Samantha tried to edge closer to hear more. But two of the children in front of her started arguing, and their shrill voices blocked out everything else.

The line moved forward through heavy doors, and Samantha started up the steps. The wedge-shaped stairs wound up the tower like a corkscrew, and Samantha couldn't see anyone but the French children directly ahead of her.

This is like climbing the Eiffel Tower, Samantha thought. But fortunately, these stairs were enclosed in the tower, and she didn't have to look at the ground below. She just had to keep climbing.

After what seemed like forever, the stairs branched off, and Samantha realized that she had to make a choice. Visitors could step outside along a balcony to see the gargoyles. Or they could continue to climb to the top of the tower. She saw the French family exit the stairs at the balcony, but she didn't know which way William and Frederick had gone.

For a moment she hesitated. Then she heard William's voice from above her: "Are you sure you want to do this, Fred? It could be dangerous for you."

"I'm sure," Frederick replied. He sounded out of breath.

They must be headed for the top of the tower, thought Samantha. Forgetting all caution, she climbed, too. She listened hard for hints of their conversation. All she heard was the sound of boots on the stairs.

Finally, she felt a rush of cold air. She knew she must be close to the top. But when she walked out, she gasped. There below her was a stunning view of Paris and the river.

Staring down, Samantha suddenly felt dizzy. She took a step back from the edge. A stern voice asked, "Samantha, is something wrong?"

She looked up. William and Frederick were right in front of her, their tall forms outlined against the sky. *What if William realizes I was following them?* Samantha thought in a panic.

"You're as white as a sheet," said William. "Do you feel sick?"

"I'm fine," Samantha said quickly. Being careful

not to look down again, she added, "I just didn't realize how high we are."

Frederick nodded. "It is beautiful up here, isn't it?"
he said, gazing out by the edge of the rooftop. "I like
it every bit as much as the Eiffel Tower."

Then a sudden gust of wind buffeted them.
Frederick reached for his hat, but before he could
grab it, Samantha saw his thick dark hair shift side-
ways on his head.

She caught her breath. *Is Frederick wearing a wig?*

William scowled at her. "You don't look well,"
he said gruffly. "You should sit down."

"No, no, I have to go," Samantha stuttered nervously. She turned away and raced down the stairs,
only pausing to be sure that William and Frederick
weren't following her.

She didn't stop to catch her breath until she was
back inside the cathedral. She found Nellie standing underneath a stained-glass window near the
back of the church. Her heart pounding, Samantha

told her sister what she'd overheard in the tower. "William and Frederick are both keeping secrets," she concluded. "And there's something else—I think Frederick is wearing a wig!"

"How strange!" whispered Nellie, her eyes wide. She lowered her voice even more. "I've been trying to stay near Ingrid, but she keeps running after Bertie—and avoiding me." Nellie turned to look for the nanny. "Oh no, Samantha, now she and Bertie are coming this way. I hope she didn't see me watching her."

Bertie ran past them. "Bertie, don't run in church," Ingrid instructed. Bertie slowed only slightly.

As Ingrid headed toward the girls, her face was clouded with worry. Samantha held her breath. *Does Ingrid know that Nellie and I suspect her?*

Ingrid stopped just inches away from them. She looked around and then said quickly in a low voice, "I'm sorry I lied this morning, Nellie. I've felt bad about it ever since. It *was* me you saw on the stairs last night. But please don't tell Mr. and Mrs. Vanderhoff. I can't let them know I went to the opera."

"The opera?" Samantha repeated in surprise. "That's where you went?"

"Yes!" Ingrid whispered. She glanced down the aisle. Bertie had joined his parents and the rest of the group near the front of the church. "William decided to stay at the hotel, so Frederick asked if I'd go with him to the opera. Monsieur LeBlanc and his wife went, too, because he had the tickets that the Vanderhoffs didn't want. Frederick and I were with Monsieur LeBlanc and his wife the whole time, so it was quite proper." Ingrid smiled. "And I had a lovely evening!"

"But the Vanderhoffs didn't know?" asked Nellie as a clump of tourists passed by.

"No, they'd never have let me go," Ingrid admitted. "But they all went to sleep early, and my room is near the door, so they didn't hear me leave." Ingrid hesitated. "I know it was wrong for me to sneak out, but I'm twenty-four, and I'd never been to an opera before—and I did so want to see it. Please don't tell Mr. and Mrs. Vanderhoff!"

Ingrid looked toward the front of the church again. "Oh, no! Bertie is trying to pick up the candles!" she exclaimed and rushed away.

"I guess that explains why Ingrid had mud on her shoes," whispered Nellie as the two girls headed down the aisle to rejoin Monsieur LeBlanc's group.

"There's something else, though," Samantha said as she saw William and Frederick gather with the rest of their tour group. "Why did William buy a ticket for the opera and then decide not to go? He and Frederick are definitely hiding something. We have to find out what it is."

Thin Ice

"NOW I CAN tell you about the surprise I have for you today," announced Monsieur LeBlanc after they left Notre-Dame Cathedral and had a late lunch at a café.

"Paris is rarely cold enough for skating, but today has turned out to be perfect!" he said as the omnibus rolled through the icy streets. "So we will visit the *Bois de Boulogne*. Centuries ago, it was a forest where kings hunted. Now it's a magnificent park, and in winter, it has a skating pond. Long ago, Emperor Napoleon himself once skated there. Today, I'll rent skates for anyone who'd like to enjoy the ice."

"I love skating!" shouted Bertie.

Monsieur LeBlanc asked who else would like to join the skating party. Ingrid eagerly raised her hand.

Then Frederick's hand shot up. William cast a side-long glance at his cousin before slowly raising his hand, too.

Mrs. Gray said that she would take Prince for a walk around the park instead of skating. But Mr. and Mrs. Vanderhoff decided they would stay at the hotel. "It's been a busy day, and my nerves need to rest," said Mrs. Vanderhoff, fanning her face. "Ingrid, you'll watch over Bertie, won't you?"

"Yes, ma'am," promised Ingrid.

The omnibus pulled up in front of the Imperial Excelsior Hotel, and Monsieur LeBlanc jumped out. "We'll meet in the lobby in half an hour. Remember to dress warmly. It will be cold on the pond."

As Samantha and Nellie entered their hotel suite, Doris told them that they had missed their grand-mother. "She's back at the hospital now, but she had good news. The Admiral is coming home tonight!"

"Hurrah!" Samantha cheered.

"That is good news!" agreed Nellie.

Doris nodded enthusiastically. "And luckily, your grandmother missed the fire alarm today, too."

Samantha's eyes widened. "There was a fire alarm?"

"Yes indeed," said Doris. "The fire bells started ringing around ten this morning. Everyone had to leave the hotel for a good hour or more. Luckily, I was able to wait in the bakery next door, or I would've frozen to death." Doris shook her head. "And after all that fuss, it turned out to be a false alarm."

Nellie asked if anyone besides Grandmary had been in the suite while they were gone.

"Only the hotel maid, Claire," Doris replied. "And I watched her like a hawk the whole time she was here to make sure she cleaned properly."

When the girls were inside their bedroom, Nellie whispered to Samantha, "Do you think the thief might have set off the fire alarm on purpose—just so he could search the suite?"

"Maybe," said Samantha, looking around uneasily. It was frightening to think that someone could have been searching their room. The girls looked around to see if anything had been moved.

Nellie pointed to the crate. "I think that was closer to the window before. Of course, Claire might have moved it when she cleaned."

"I hope all the gifts are still in the crate," said Samantha.

Together, she and Nellie opened the wooden crate and checked through the gifts. The parasol and walking stick were still packed on either side of the Eiffel Tower replica, which was wrapped in brown paper. But Samantha saw that the note she had written to Bridget and Jenny saying "SECRET" was no longer in the center of the wrapping paper.

"That's odd," said Samantha, finding the note in the corner of the box. "The note isn't where I left it— and the wrapping paper looks crumpled, too. Let's look inside."

She and Nellie took off the brown paper and checked through the drawers in the model's base. Samantha leafed through the postcards that Nellie had hidden inside the drawers. "I guess it's all right," she said. "I think all the postcards are here."

She was about to put the postcards back in the drawers when Nellie said, "Wait!"

Nellie studied the stack of cards for a moment, and then she looked at Samantha, her face white. "When I put these cards in, I wanted Bridget and Jenny to see the one with the Eiffel Tower on it first, so I put that postcard on top. But now it's in the middle. Did you move it?"

"No."

"Are you sure?"

"Positive." Samantha had a sickening feeling in her stomach as she stared down at the open crate. "Nellie, someone has been in here!"

"William was missing from the tour this morning," Nellie whispered. "The fire alarm began ringing at ten. So he would have had time to come in here while we were all at the museum."

Samantha recalled William and Frederick's conversation in the tower. She whispered back, "Maybe William and Frederick are *both* thieves, and they are working together."

The girls heard Doris talking in the sitting room. Then Doris knocked on their door. "Girls, Mrs. Gray stopped by. She said to tell you that the group is leaving to go skating soon."

Samantha bit her lip. She'd been excited about skating, and now, more than ever, she wanted to keep close watch on William and Frederick. But she was determined not to leave Doris alone in the suite again.

"Nellie, why don't you go? I'll stay here and look for the letter," she offered.

"No, Samantha, *I'll* stay here," Nellie said firmly. "I start coughing when I'm out in the cold wind."

"If you're going, you'd better hurry!" Doris called

from the sitting room. "And wear your warmest stockings, too."

The skating pond at the Bois de Boulogne looked like a winter fairyland. Trees, their branches glittering with ice, surrounded the big pond, which was busy with skaters of all ages. Samantha saw ladies wearing large hats, little children struggling to stand, and even a group of French soldiers, laughing and skating together.

Mrs. Gray took Prince, who was now dressed in a handsome blue jacket and matching ribbon, for a walk around the pond, while William, Frederick, Ingrid, Bertie, and Samantha all went with Monsieur LeBlanc to rent skates.

Samantha was last in line, and when she finally got her skates, she sat down on a bench and buckled the runners tightly over her shoes. Then she wobbled to the pond's edge and set off across the ice, the wind blowing in her hair as she glided over the frozen pond.

She skated in circles and traced figures in the ice, trying to keep an eye on both William and Frederick while seeming as if she was just enjoying weaving through the crowds of skaters.

"You're quite a good skater, Samantha," said Monsieur LeBlanc, who skated by as she was doing figure eights. "But take care to avoid the thin ice over there." He pointed to a sign at the far end of the pond, where no one was skating.

"I will," said Samantha. As Monsieur LeBlanc skated away, Samantha looked over at William, who was gliding around the pond, his hands clasped behind his back. The big man's skating looked effortless, but he was passing everyone else.

Samantha turned around and skated backward as she watched Frederick and Ingrid skate nearby, with Ingrid holding Bertie by the hand.

Ingrid skated gracefully, her long skirts flowing

behind her like a swan's wings. Bertie seemed at home on the ice, too. But Frederick was moving awkwardly, and he seemed unsure on his feet.

That's odd, thought Samantha. *I'd think that a Canadian would know how to skate.*

Frederick was going so slowly that Bertie became impatient. The little boy jerked his hand away from Ingrid's and started skating away on his own.

Samantha heard Ingrid cry, "Bertie, come back here!"

Ingrid sounded unusually upset. Samantha glanced over her shoulder to see what the little boy was doing. She gasped as she saw that Bertie was headed for the thin ice.

Samantha whirled around. Pushing off hard with her skates, she started after Bertie, racing to get to him in time. But Ingrid was already ahead of her, chasing after the little boy, with Frederick in close pursuit.

"Bertie, stop! Don't go any farther," Ingrid shouted.

But Bertie kept speeding toward the part of the pond where there was no one else around.

Samantha's heart pounded as she skated. She realized that Bertie would never understand the French sign for thin ice. *We have to stop him before he falls through the ice!*

Bertie was flying ahead, though, and he was so small that he was easily able to thread his way around the other skaters. Ingrid and Frederick were still behind him, but Frederick was going fast now, as if he'd remembered how to skate. He passed Ingrid, and as he neared the boy, he yelled, "Bertie, stop!"

But Bertie had crossed over to the thin ice. Frederick crunched to a halt near the sign. He and Ingrid called to Bertie to come back.

Samantha arrived breathless at the edge of the solid ice. She saw Bertie turn around. He was smiling, as if proud that he'd won a race. Then, as he started to push off with one skate, his rear foot fell through the ice. He stumbled forward and fell, arms reaching out.

"Ingrid, help!" he screamed. "The ice is breaking!"

He could fall through and drown! Samantha thought with horror.

"Bertie, don't stand up," commanded Frederick. "Stretch out over the ice, as if you're making a snow angel."

Samantha saw Bertie look up uncertainly. But Frederick's voice held a note of authority, and Bertie obeyed, gingerly stretching his limbs out over the thin ice.

To Samantha's relief, as Bertie spread out his weight, the ice seemed to hold him. "I'll go get him," she said, starting forward.

Frederick grabbed her shoulder. "No! Don't step out there. I don't want two people sinking." He took off his coat and hat.

William raced up, his blades scraping as he turned in a tight stop. "Fred, let me do this," he said.

"No, I'll go," Frederick insisted. "I'm so thin now

that I weigh a lot less than you, Will." Frederick fell
to his knees and, with his coat in his hand, started to
crawl carefully toward Bertie. He called back to his
cousin. "You get my legs, Will."

"I'M COLD!" Bertie cried.

"Stay there, Bertie," Ingrid reassured the child.
"Frederick is coming for you."

A small crowd of skaters began to gather nearby,
and Monsieur LeBlanc said something to them in
French. A man hurried away, as if to get help.

Samantha could hardly take her eyes off Bertie.
Alone on the ice, the little boy looked terrified. *They
have to get to him soon!*

As Frederick eased his way on all fours across
the thin ice, William crouched behind him.

"I've got you, Fred," William said. He held one
of Frederick's legs, making a human chain from the
solid ice to the thin area. Several French soldiers
gathered behind William, ready to come to the
rescue if needed.

Samantha held her breath as the ice creaked beneath Frederick. When he got within a few feet of Bertie, Frederick spread out on the ice and extended his coat to the little boy. "Grab it and hold tight," he told him.

Bertie grasped the coat, and Frederick pulled him toward the solid ice. There was a round of cheers when they were both finally safe. William took off his own coat, covered Bertie with it, and carried him to the waiting omnibus. Frederick picked up his hat and coat, and then he, Ingrid, and Samantha followed close behind.

While Monsieur LeBlanc went to find Mrs. Gray, Samantha helped Ingrid wrap Bertie in a carriage blanket and dry the foot that had fallen in icy water. William looked at Bertie's foot and said that he didn't think it was frostbitten. "Bertie, you were lucky," William said, wrapping him in the blanket again.

"Thank you so much, Frederick! And you, too, William," Ingrid gushed. "Bertie, say 'Thank you.'

Frederick saved you!"

"Thank you," said Bertie, as Frederick and William sat down on the opposite bench. Then Bertie looked quizzically at Frederick. "Why is your hair falling off?"

Samantha glanced over and saw that Frederick's dark hair was now tilted on his scalp. Frederick quickly put his hat on his head, but it was too late.

It is a wig! thought Samantha.

Her heart fell. During Bertie's rescue, Samantha had been so worried about the little boy that she had pushed aside her suspicions about Frederick and William. Now all her fears came flooding back.

Samantha saw Frederick and William exchange a glance.

Then Frederick took off his hat. "Please let me explain," he said slowly.

chapter 13

Trapped

WHEN SAMANTHA RETURNED to the
hotel suite, Nellie answered the door. "You're back
early," said Nellie, surprised. Then she added in a low
voice, "I looked for the letter, but I didn't find anything."

"I found out a lot," said Samantha. "Come on, let's
go to our room."

As soon as the door was closed behind them,
Samantha sank down on her bed and told Nellie
about Bertie's rescue at the pond and the discovery
of Frederick's wig.

"Frederick and William both have secrets,"
Samantha said finally.

"What are they?" asked Nellie, sitting up straight.

"Frederick told us that he was in the hospital last
fall with a terrible fever," Samantha explained. "All his

hair fell out, and that's why he wears a wig now. The reason he came on this trip was because he needed time to recover. And William is a doctor in Toronto. He's been watching over his cousin to make sure he doesn't get sick again."

Nellie frowned. "William told us that he was a geologist."

"Yes, he says that his hobby is geology, and he didn't want everyone asking him medical questions while he was on holiday, so he just decided to say he was a geologist. But after the Admiral fell, William felt bad that he hadn't told the truth earlier. He visited the Admiral in the hospital because he was worried about his injuries."

"I bet if she'd known he was a doctor, Mrs. Vanderhoff would've asked William all about her nerves!" said Nellie, smiling. Then she looked serious again. "But if William and Frederick aren't the thieves, we don't have any idea who is trying to steal the secret letter."

"I know," Samantha agreed. She got up and took the group photograph from the wardrobe. "It has to be someone from our tour," she said, examining the photograph again. "But I don't see how it could be *anyone* in this picture."

"How about someone who isn't in the picture?" suggested Nellie. "I like Monsieur LeBlanc, but he *was* behind the Admiral on the path, and he could've sneaked up on him."

Samantha shook her head. "Ingrid said that she and Frederick spent all of last evening at the opera with Monsieur LeBlanc and his wife. So Monsieur LeBlanc *couldn't* have been the person we heard searching our suite."

There was a knock on the door, and then Doris stepped into the room. She was wearing her coat and carrying a basket over her arm. "When your grandmother was here, she asked me to shop for a few things. I'll be back as soon as I can. You girls come and bolt the door after I leave."

Samantha and Nellie followed Doris to the entry. As Doris opened the door, Mrs. Gray's maid, Martha, walked by. She was dressed in her coat and hat and held a basket in her hand. She gave the girls a sharp glance as she passed their door. Then she nodded and, with a thin smile, moved on.

"I guess she's shopping, too," said Doris with a sigh. "Well, wish me luck, girls, and don't let anyone in while I'm gone."

Samantha closed the door and bolted it immediately. She'd had the strange feeling that Martha had been observing them closely.

"What about Martha?" Samantha whispered to Nellie. "We don't know anything about her, really. Maybe she's just pretending to be a maid. She could be the thief."

"It couldn't be Martha—she wasn't even in the catacombs," said Nellie, frowning. "Mrs. Gray sent her back to the hotel with Prince, remember?"

But Samantha's mind was spinning with new

suspicions. She began pacing across the sitting room. "What if Martha left Prince somewhere and then went into the catacombs before we even got there?" Samantha turned to face Nellie. "Martha knew that's where we were going, and the tunnel is so dark that we wouldn't have recognized Martha if we'd walked right past her. She could have followed us and waited until the Admiral was alone." Samantha felt a shiver go up her back at the terrible thought.

"Maybe..." Nellie replied. She sat down on the sofa as Samantha continued to pace. "But Mrs. Gray said that Martha was asleep in her room last night when we heard someone come into the sitting room. And whoever came into our sitting room went into Mrs. Gray's suite, too."

Samantha continued to pace, thinking back to what Mrs. Gray had told them about the previous night. "Mrs. Gray never looked into Martha's room, did she?" Samantha said as her shoes clicked on the floor. "What if it was Martha we heard in here last night—and when she left, she went back to Mrs. Gray's suite? Mrs. Gray thought someone was breaking in, but it might've been Martha coming *back in*."

"You're right, Samantha." Nellie stood up and looked around the room uneasily. "Martha *could* have sneaked back into Mrs. Gray's suite. Ingrid said it was easy for her to leave the Vanderhoffs' without anyone noticing—Martha could've done the same thing."

Samantha nodded. "Nellie, we have to find out more about Martha," she said, heading for the door. "Let's go talk to Mrs. Gray."

"Won't she wonder why we're asking?"

"Mrs. Gray said to come by whenever we wanted to," said Samantha as she stepped out into the hall. "We'll just say hello."

"Wait for me," Nellie said. She hurried back to their room and came back with the long iron key. "I'll lock the door while we're gone."

When Samantha knocked at 404, Claire, the hotel chambermaid, opened the door. Next to Claire was the sweeper she used to clean floors, and Samantha could hear Prince barking in another room.

"Hello, Claire," Nellie said. "May we speak with Mrs. Gray, please?"

"I'll go get her," said Claire cheerfully.

A moment later, the young widow appeared at the door. She'd changed since their trip to the park, and now she was wearing a black traveling suit trimmed with lace. "It's a pleasure to see you girls," she said, stepping out into the hall. "I'm sorry that I can't invite you in right now, since the maid is cleaning. Is there anything I can help you with?" Mrs. Gray smiled. "Has your grandfather returned?"

"He's not back yet, but we expect him soon," said Samantha. She felt her face flush as Mrs. Gray looked at her expectantly.

Samantha shifted uneasily from one foot to the other, not sure how to bring up Martha in the conversation. Finally, she began, "We just saw Martha. It looked as if she was going shopping."

Mrs. Gray smiled again. "Yes, was there something you'd like her to buy for you? I could ask her
when she gets back."

"Oh, that's all right," said Samantha quickly.
She felt hot with embarrassment. "We were just
wondering—"

Nellie interjected, "Has Martha worked for you
a long time?"

"Why, no," Mrs. Gray said. "I hired her just last
week when I was in London." The widow put her
hand to the delicate lace around her throat. "Dear me,
Martha hasn't done anything wrong, has she? She
came highly recommended."

"No," said Samantha. "I mean, we don't know of
anything she's done wrong." Samantha felt her face
turn even hotter as Mrs. Gray studied her. Was it her
imagination, or did Mrs. Gray suspect something too?

"We'd better go," said Nellie abruptly. "Thank you."

Together, Nellie and Samantha fled back to their
hotel suite. "I'm sorry, Nellie!" Samantha said as soon

as the door was closed behind them. "I thought it would be easy to ask questions, but it was hard to talk while we were standing out there in the hall."

"At least we found out something," said Nellie thoughtfully. "Martha has worked for Mrs. Gray for only a short time."

Samantha and Nellie discussed what to do next. "Let's go talk to Mrs. Gray again," Samantha urged. "We'd better ask her not to tell Martha that we had questions about her. Martha could get suspicious."

"Samantha, I don't think that's a good idea," Nellie warned. "Martha could return any moment."

"We just need to get there before Martha does," said Samantha. "Come on—let's go!"

When they returned to Suite 404, Claire opened the door again. Samantha could hear Prince barking somewhere in the suite. Claire said, "I'm sorry. Mrs. Gray just stepped out. She told me she'd be right back. Would you like to come inside and wait for her?"

"Yes, please," said Samantha.

She and Nellie sat on the blue satin couch while Claire finished tidying the sitting room. As the maid emptied a trash basket into a bin, a shiny paper fell to the floor. Samantha leaned over and picked it up. It was the bright silvered paper used to wrap sweets and sugared almonds.

Samantha glanced into the bin and saw lots more of the little papers. They looked just like the ones Ingrid had found in the catacombs. Samantha felt the hairs on the back of her neck quiver. *Could it be just a coincidence?* she wondered. *Or did Martha leave those wrappers in the catacombs?*

As Claire pushed the sweeper toward the entry, Samantha whispered, "Did you see those wrappers?"

"Yes." Nellie looked around uneasily. "I hope Mrs. Gray gets back soon."

Claire stepped back into the sitting room. "I'll be

going now, but I'm sure Mrs. Gray won't mind if you girls wait here."

Samantha heard Prince still barking. The sound seemed to come from the servant's bedroom off the entry hall. "May we let Prince out?"

Claire shook her head. "No, I feel quite sorry for the poor dog, but Mrs. Gray says he's not allowed out of that room. It's kept locked so that he can't push his way out. I'm not even allowed to clean in there."

The front door closed behind Claire, and Prince's barking became even more desperate. "He sounds so unhappy," said Nellie, worried. "He must be lonely."

Samantha nodded. She couldn't listen to that sad barking any longer without trying to comfort the dog. "If he's not supposed to come out of the room, let's visit him in there," she suggested. She stood up and started toward the door.

Nellie hesitated. "I don't know, Samantha. Do you think Mrs. Gray would mind?"

"I think Mrs. Gray will be glad that we cheered Prince up," Samantha encouraged her. "And we'll be very quick—we'll just say hello to him."

Nellie nodded reluctantly, and together they followed the sound of barking to the servant's bedroom. The room was locked from the outside, but the iron key was still in the lock. Samantha turned the key and stepped into the room.

"Jiminy!" Samantha exclaimed. Like Doris's room, this small bedroom had a single bed, an ironing board, and a tall window flanked by long white curtains. But while Doris's room was neat and sparkling clean, this bedroom looked as if only Prince had been shut inside it—and no one had cleaned it in a long time. There were crumpled newspapers on the floor and an empty bowl in the corner.

Prince jumped up on Samantha, whining. He was no longer dressed in the handsome blue jacket and ribbon he'd worn to the Bois de Boulogne. He had just an old leather collar around his neck.

"Hello there, boy!" Samantha said, kneeling down to pat the frantic dog. "What's the matter?"

Nellie came into the room and closed the door behind her. She looked down at the bowl. "Prince must be thirsty," she said. "I don't see any water here for him—or food either."

Samantha stood up, her stomach tight with fear. "Nellie, something's wrong. I thought Mrs. Gray loved Prince. Why does she leave him locked up in here with dirty newspapers and no water?"

Instead of answering, Nellie put a finger up. "Someone's here," she whispered.

Samantha paused and listened. She heard a door shut in the entry hall. Prince started barking again.

A woman shouted, "Oh, be quiet, you stupid dog!"

Prince shrank back into a corner, suddenly silent.

Martha is back! Samantha thought. *And Prince is scared of her.*

A moment later, she heard the entry door open again. Another woman said, "Hurry up and pack.

Those girls suspect you—it's only a matter of time before they tell someone. We have to get out of here."

It was Mrs. Gray, but her voice sounded harsh and cold. Samantha's stomach dropped as she realized that Mrs. Gray and Martha were not at all who they'd pretended to be. *They're the thieves, and they're working together!*

Nellie's eyes widened with fear. She looked as horrified as Samantha felt.

Samantha heard Martha say, "What about the letter? We won't be paid if we don't get it, and this will all have been a waste of time. Vanderhoff's wallet barely covered our expenses."

"It's a good thing I did get that wallet!" Mrs. Gray replied sharply. "Now it's too late for the letter. Did you get everything I told you to?"

"Yes, as usual I've had to do all the work! I got the tickets *and* your seasickness pills," Martha grumbled.

"Stop complaining. We need to get packed," Mrs. Gray snapped. "We don't have much time."

The girls heard the tap of a woman's shoes. Someone was walking down the entry hall. "Hide!" whispered Nellie.

Nellie crept behind the bed, and Samantha followed her. They both crouched down, making themselves as small as possible.

Prince started barking at the girls in their hiding place. "Shh!" Samantha hushed him. Prince just barked louder.

The door to the little bedroom opened, and Prince ran to it, barking. "At least we never have to see you again, you stupid dog!" Martha shouted, shoving Prince with her foot. "Now be quiet!" She banged the door shut again. Prince whimpered.

How dare she treat Prince that way! Samantha thought furiously.

Then Samantha heard the key click in the lock on the other side. She felt her heart thudding. *We're trapped!*

chapter 14

Escape

"WE HAVE TO get help!" Nellie whispered.

Samantha looked desperately around the room. The only door was locked. She parted the window curtains and peered out. There was no fire escape or balcony, just the street far below.

The setting sun cast a red glow on nearby buildings. Samantha could see flags flying and lights beginning to be lit for the evening. Carriages and automobiles rushed along the busy street, and people bundled up in winter coats hurried back and forth along the sidewalk.

If only we could get someone's attention, Samantha thought. She looked again at the flags snapping in the wind and the curtains hanging by the window. *Maybe we could make our own flag . . .*

Samantha checked her pockets. They were empty. She whispered, "Nellie, do you have a pencil?"

Nellie felt inside her pockets and pulled out her handkerchief. Tucked inside it were some of the chocolates that the Admiral had given them. "This is all I have."

It's just like Nellie to save her chocolates, thought Samantha, staring down at the wrapped squares. *But I wish they were crayons instead.*

Then Samantha had an idea. She whispered to Nellie.

Nellie nodded, and as quietly as possible, the girls pulled one of the long white curtains off the curtain rod and put it over the ironing board. Then Samantha unwrapped a chocolate square, licked it, and tried using it like a crayon to draw a line down the curtain.

To her immense relief, the chocolate made a thick, heavy line that was easy to see against the white cloth. Nellie unwrapped another piece of chocolate and began writing across the curtain, too. Together, they spelled out in dark letters about three feet high:

HELP

Then the girls eased the big window open. A blast of cold air rushed in. Prince stopped barking and stood at the girls' feet. The dog watched intently as they reached out the window and held up their homemade flag.

After a few moments, Nellie choked back a cough. "I'm sorry," she whispered, gasping for breath. "It's the wind."

"Wait by the door," Samantha whispered back. "Tell me if you hear anything."

Now Samantha was on her own. She leaned out the window as far as she could without risking falling. She felt queasy as she looked at the ground below, but she steadied herself and took a deep breath. Then she kept on waving the flag with all her strength, even as her hands started to go numb from the cold.

Nellie whispered urgently, "Samantha, they're about to leave!"

Please someone help us! Samantha prayed silently. Her arms were getting tired, and soon it would be dark. If she and Nellie were left locked in here, it could be hours till anyone found them. By then, Mrs. Gray and Martha would be far away.

"Samantha!" Nellie whispered excitedly. "I hear banging at the door!"

Pulling the flag inside, Samantha hurried over and stood beside Nellie, listening. With a rush of joy, she heard a familiar voice declare imperiously, "Don't be absurd! I know my granddaughters are in here. Now step out of my way. Monsieur Andreyev, please restrain these women!"

Nellie and Samantha pounded on the door. "Grandmary!" they shouted. "We're in here!"

A moment later, Grandmary had unlocked the

door from the other side. "Oh, my dear, dear girls!" she exclaimed. She put her arms around them both, holding them close. "I saw that flag and I knew it must be you. Are you all right?"

"Yes, Grandmary," Nellie reassured her. "Yes, we're fine, now!" Both girls hugged their grandmother again, while Prince danced around them, barking excitedly.

Then Samantha pulled away and started for the door. "We have to stop Mrs. Gray and Martha!" she told Grandmary. "They're thieves—and they're the ones who robbed the Admiral."

"You and Nellie stay right here with me, Samantha," said Grandmary firmly. "Those women ran out as soon as I came in. Monsieur Andreyev and his men are pursuing them now."

A few minutes later, Prince barked as the hotel manager returned to the suite. Monsieur Andreyev told them that the two women had escaped, but he'd called the police. "They ran away without paying the bill!" he declared, mopping his brow.

"They did worse than that," Samantha said, patting Prince. Careful not to reveal anything about the Admiral's secret, Samantha and Nellie explained that the women they'd known as Mrs. Gray and her maid, Martha, were actually thieves who were working together.

"They stole from our grandfather and Mr. Vanderhoff in the catacombs," Nellie said.

"Well, we know where those two are going," said Monsieur Andreyev, puffing out his chest proudly. "This afternoon, Mrs. Gray asked the desk clerk for train schedules to Rome. The police will check all the trains to Italy."

Nellie said slowly, "Maybe they were trying to fool everyone by asking about the trains."

The hotel manager turned to Nellie, frowning. "Why do you say that?"

"Because Mrs. Gray gets seasick like I do, and she made sure she had seasickness medicine before she left," Nellie said. "I think she's planning to travel on a ship."

"It's something to consider," admitted Monsieur Andreyev, stroking his mustache. "I'll tell the police to look for them at the seaports, too."

As he hurried away, Grandmary put her arms around the girls' shoulders. "Let's go back to our suite," she said. "There's someone who wants to see you, and you can tell us everything that happened."

"Can Prince come too?" asked Samantha, still holding the little dog in her arms. "They left him here without any food or water."

Grandmary nodded. "Bring him along. Doris will get him something to eat."

"We'll give you some food!" Samantha whispered to Prince as they walked down the hall, and the spaniel wagged his tail.

Inside their suite, they found the Admiral resting on the sofa. He'd taken off his coat and set his hat and walking stick beside him. The only sign of his injury was a white bandage above one eyebrow. Samantha and Nellie rushed to hug him.

"Jolly good to see you again, my dears!" he exclaimed, giving them each a kiss on the forehead. "When we returned, we found that you were gone. Your grandmother and I wondered what had become of you."

"I wondered, too!" said Doris as she served them tea and sandwiches. "Don't ever disappear like that again!"

Samantha and Nellie fed bits of their sandwiches to Prince. As the little dog ate eagerly, the girls told their grandparents how they'd become trapped in Suite 404.

Grandmary replied by giving them a spirited lecture. She concluded by telling them to never, ever go off on such a dangerous errand again.

"It was my fault," Samantha confessed. "Nellie didn't think it was a good idea to go to Mrs. Gray's suite, but I talked her into it."

Grandmary nodded approvingly at Nellie, and then she sighed. "Well," she said, relaxing slightly. "I'm glad you're both safe now."

"How did you find us, Grandmary?" asked Samantha.

"When I discovered that you were missing, I looked downstairs in the lobby and the reading room, and then I stepped outside. I thought perhaps Monsieur LeBlanc's omnibus might be there. As I was walking back in, your flag caught my eye. I saw a girl waving it. I couldn't see the face clearly, but I was sure it must be one of you girls."

"Why?" Nellie asked.

"You were on the top floor, near our suite, and the flag said 'Help' in English." Grandmary smiled. "A French girl would have asked for help in French."

"Of course!" said Samantha. She shook her head regretfully. "I always forget to use French!"

Nellie fed Prince another tidbit of sandwich. "Admiral, do you think Mrs. Gray ever really cared about Prince?"

"No," said the Admiral. He leaned forward and stroked the dog's head. "I believe she simply used him as a prop. She probably wanted an excuse to introduce herself and find out where we were staying."

And she made up the story about hearing an intruder in her suite, too, Samantha thought. *She knew we'd heard someone, and she didn't want us to suspect her!*

"I can't believe I fell into her trap," said Grandmary, shaking her head. "But she seemed so pleasant."

"Mrs. Gray and Martha are a skillful pair of thieves," said the Admiral. "They had me fooled, too."

"But you did try to warn us in the catacombs!" Nellie said. "Remember? When Samantha and I found you on the ground, you said, 'Be careful.' Then you said something about the tour. You probably suspected Martha and Mrs. Gray even then."

"Yes," said Samantha, thinking back to that awful time. "Mrs. Gray and Martha must have planned everything together. Mrs. Gray called to us, while

Martha stole your wallet."

The Admiral shook his head regretfully. "I'm afraid I still don't remember how I came to be injured. But perhaps something *had* made me suspicious." There was a loud knock on the door. "Ah, that will be the visitor I was expecting."

Doris went to answer the door. When she returned, her eyes were wide. "Admiral Beemis, sir, the British ambassador is here to see you!"

She ushered a tall, distinguished-looking gentleman into the room. He was followed by the red-haired man Samantha had seen in the reading room and three other solemn men in business suits. The Admiral stood up and shook hands with them.

"Good to see you, Archie! It's been too long," the ambassador said.

The Admiral introduced Grandmary, Nellie, and Samantha. As she did her best curtsy, Samantha wondered, *Why is the British ambassador here?*

The ambassador told the other men to wait in the

hall and then settled himself on the chair across from the Admiral.

"Would you like us to wait elsewhere?" Grand-mary asked the Admiral.

"No, my dear," he replied. "I believe that you and Nellie and Samantha have earned the right to be part of this meeting."

"I just returned from Belgium and got your message, Archie. I came straightaway," said the ambassador. "Was your meeting with the Russians successful? Did they agree to sign the letter?"

"Yes," said the Admiral. "But other countries must have learned about the letter, because two thieves were hired to steal it." The Admiral smiled. "Thanks to my granddaughters, however, the police have been alerted and are now searching for the thieves. Perhaps someday we'll find out who they were working for."

The ambassador leaned forward in his chair. "You have the signed letter, though, don't you? It wasn't stolen?"

"The letter never left my side," said the Admiral. "I was just waiting for your return to give it to you." He reached for his walking stick and unscrewed the gold handle. Then, from a hidden compartment inside the stick, he pulled out a tightly rolled paper. The Admiral unrolled the paper and handed it to the ambassador.

So that's why the Admiral asked for his walking stick in the catacombs, thought Samantha. *The letter was inside it!*

The ambassador skimmed the letter. "Thank heavens!" he sighed.

He carefully placed the letter in his briefcase. Then he stood up. "This document must remain a secret for now, but on behalf of our king and country, I give you our deepest thanks." He bowed formally and said good-bye.

"Well, girls," said the Admiral after the ambassador left. "We have thanks from England. That's something to take home with us, even though we'll never be able to talk about it."

Samantha hesitated. "What about Prince?" she asked. The spaniel, having eaten his fill, was now lying peacefully on the floor in front of her. "Could we take him home with us? Those women were mean to him, and we can't just leave him here..."

Grandmary and the Admiral looked at each other. "He *is* a nice little dog," said Grandmary slowly.

"Very well," said the Admiral, leaning down to pat Prince. "We'll bring him home and you girls can see him when you visit us." The Admiral looked up. "As for going home, though, I'm afraid..."

"We must sail back to New York earlier than we'd planned," Grandmary finished the sentence for him. "The doctors want your grandfather to rest for a few days, and the sea voyage would be a good opportunity for that. So we shall be leaving the day after tomorrow."

"We understand," Samantha said.

"Yes," Nellie agreed quickly. "Paris is beautiful,

but it will be nice to see everyone at home again, too."

"I'm glad you don't mind too much," said the Admiral, looking relieved. "And your grandmother and I would like to invite you girls to come with us on another trip to Europe next summer. We'll have sun and warm breezes then, and the gardens will all be in bloom. We'll invite Bridget and Jenny, too."

Nellie stared at him for a moment, speechless. "You would do that—bring all of us?"

"Of course," said Grandmary, smiling. "We're all a family now."

"And we'll have grand adventures together!" declared the Admiral.

Tears of happiness filled Samantha's eyes as Nellie hugged both the Admiral and Grandmary. "I'm so glad to be your granddaughter," Nellie said, wiping away tears of her own. "So very glad!"

· · ·

The next morning, the Admiral, Grandmary, Nellie, and Samantha all went down to the hotel restaurant for breakfast, and they joined the Vanderhoffs and Ingrid at a big table. Monsieur Andreyev came into the dining room to tell them that he'd heard from the police. "The women who pretended to be Mrs. Gray and her maid Martha are actually sisters. They're well-known thieves, and they are wanted by the police in several countries."

"I'm not surprised!" declared Mrs. Vanderhoff. She set down her coffee cup with a clatter. "I suspected that nasty Mrs. Gray from the very beginning! She never fooled me for a moment."

Nellie and Samantha shared a glance, and Samantha tried hard not to giggle.

"You were right about them taking a sea voyage, too," the hotel manager told Nellie. "They were spotted at a port last night. They are believed to be heading to Greece, and police will be waiting for them there."

"I don't suppose I'll ever get my wallet back," said

Mr. Vanderhoff with a sigh. Then he brightened. "But wait till I tell my friends in Buffalo about this!"

Suddenly Ingrid's eyes lit up and she waved happily. Samantha looked around and saw Frederick and William enter the dining room. Frederick's thatch of dark hair was gone, and he was now completely bald. But his cheeks were tinged with pink, and he smiled broadly as he walked toward them.

"I think he looks better without a wig," whispered Nellie as she put jam on her croissant.

"Me too," said Samantha.

As soon as Frederick sat down, he and Ingrid started talking and laughing together. William studied the menu.

Samantha turned toward William. One more question was bothering her. "May I ask you something?"

He looked up from his menu. "Yes?"

"Why did you buy a ticket for the opera and then not go?"

William glanced toward his cousin and then lowered his voice so that only Samantha and Nellie could hear him. "I wanted Fred to have a chance to take Ingrid. He's quite smitten with her."

"Oh, that explains it!" Samantha said. She sat back in her chair and took a sip of hot chocolate.

"If Fred was still sick at all, I think Ingrid has cured him," William continued. "And speaking of cures, about that cough of yours, Nellie..."

Nellie froze, her croissant in her hand. "Does it sound bad?"

"Well, your grandmother asked me about it, and I think perhaps the cold wind and dust in the city bother your lungs." William gulped some coffee. "I suggest you see a doctor when you get back to New York. But in the meantime, try to stay out of the wind if you can."

"That's all?" said Nellie. She looked as if she'd been prepared for much worse news. "Thank you!"

After breakfast, the Admiral and Grandmary

decided to relax in the sitting room of their suite, and
Prince happily curled up on the floor beside them.
"You go ahead with the tour today," Grandmary told
Samantha and Nellie. "Perhaps later, your grand-
father and I will take Prince for a walk along the
Champs-Élysées."

Samantha and Nellie bundled up in their coats
and met the rest of the group in the lobby. The tour-
group members were now like old friends, and
everyone was chattering. Monsieur LeBlanc clapped
his hands for their attention.

"Today I will show you more wonders of this
city!" he declared. "We have an exciting day ahead
with so much to see. Please, follow me!"

Samantha and Nellie looked at each other and
grinned. Then they started off together to enjoy one
more day in Paris.

Inside Samantha's World

In Samantha's day, many wealthy Americans made
sure that their children toured Paris and the other great
cities of Europe. These trips weren't just for fun—they
were considered an important part of a well-to-do child's
education. Parents believed they were showing their
children the height of culture and sophistication as they
toured Europe's museums, castles, and historical sites,
tried fascinating new foods, and practiced speaking
French and Italian.

The only way to reach Europe in the early 1900s was
by ship, but families like Grandmary's could sail in comfort on fast and luxurious steamships.

Once they arrived in Europe, travelers like Samantha's
family usually stayed in the finest hotels, where the
staff spoke English. Pickpockets and thieves sometimes preyed on wealthy sightseers, so a tour guide like
Monsieur LeBlanc would have provided safety as well
as convenience. A widow would also need a tour guide,
since it was considered improper for a lady to go walking
by herself, and fine restaurants would not serve a woman
sitting alone at a table!

Many of the sights that Samantha and Nellie enjoy
in the story are still "must-see" stops for tourists today.
The Eiffel Tower was built for the 1889 World's Fair in

Paris, and in Samantha's day, it was the tallest structure in the world.

The catacombs that spooked and intrigued Samantha and Nellie continue to draw thousands of tourists every year. The tunnels beneath the city were originally built for mining stone, but as Paris ran out of space for cemeteries in the late 1700s, the tunnels were converted to a vast underground burial place for old bones and skeletons. By some estimates, the catacombs hold the remains of as many as six million Parisians. In many parts of the catacombs, the bones and skulls are arranged with care and artistry to create striking effects—and in Samantha's day they were viewed by flickering candlelight!

Although it wasn't usually apparent to tourists, Europe was filled with political tensions at the turn of the twentieth century. By the time of Samantha's story in 1907, France, Great Britain, and Russia were forming an alliance and competing for power against an increasingly strong Germany and its allies. Diplomats from these countries worked in secret to further their nations' political interests. But few people in 1907 could have imagined that only seven years later, Europe's political tensions would explode into a war that spread around the world—World War One.

Glossary of French Words

Arc de Triomphe *(ahrk duh tree-ohmf)*—Arch of Triumph, a famous landmark in Paris

Bois de Boulogne *(bwah duh boo-loh-nyuh)*—a large public park in Paris

Champs-Élysées *(shahnz ay-lee-zay)*—a broad avenue leading to the Arc de Triomphe

chocolatier *(sho-kloh-tyay)*—a person who makes or sells chocolates

croissant *(kwah-sahn)*—a rich flaky pastry in the shape of a crescent

franc *(frahnk)*—money formerly used in France

kilo *(kee-loh)*—a measurement of weight, equal to about 2.3 pounds

la tour Eiffel *(lah toor eh-fel)*—the Eiffel Tower

le restaurant *(luh res-tah-rahn)*—the restaurant

madame *(mah-dahm)*—Mrs., ma'am

magnifique *(mah-nyee-feek)*—beautiful, magnificent

monsieur *(muh-syuh)*—Mr., sir

Notre-Dame *(noh-truh dahm)*—a cathedral in Paris known for its beauty

oui *(wee)*—yes

pommes frites *(pum freet)*—French fries, fried potatoes

quatre *(kah-truh)*—four

rue du Jardin *(rew dew zhahr-dahn)*—Garden Street

s'il vous plaît *(seel voo pleh)*—please

une pâtisserie *(ewn pah-tees-ree)*—a pastry

Read more of SAMANTHA'S stories,
available from booksellers and at *americangirl.com*

✎ Classics ✎
Samantha's classic series, now in two volumes:

Volume 1:
Manners and Mischief
Making friends with a servant isn't proper for a young lady— but that won't stop Samantha!

Volume 2:
Lost and Found
Samantha finally finds her friend Nellie—living in an orphanage! She's determined to help Nellie escape.

✎ Journey in Time ✎
Travel back in time—and spend a day with Samantha.

The Lilac Tunnel
What is it really like to live in Samantha's world? What if you're a servant rather than a proper young lady? Find out by choosing your own path through this multiple-ending story.

✎ Mysteries ✎
Enjoy more thrilling adventures with BeForever characters.

The Jazzman's Trumpet: A Kit Mystery
A valuable trumpet goes missing. Can Kit prove *she's* not the thief?

Secrets in the Hills: A Josefina Mystery
Could legends of ghosts and lost treasure really be true?

Shadows on Society Hill: An Addy Mystery
Addy's new home holds dangerous secrets—ones that lead straight back to the plantation she escaped from only two years before.

The Smuggler's Secrets: A Caroline Mystery
Is Caroline's uncle selling precious supplies to the enemy?

A Sneak Peek at

The Lilac Tunnel

My Journey with Samantha

Meet Samantha and take an exciting journey into
a book that lets *you* decide what happens.

here's a knock on the bedroom door. I figure it's my new stepsister, Gracie, who's been coming in and out all morning. It's her room, too, so I *have* to let her in. With a sigh, I roll off the bed and open the door. I'm surprised to see not Gracie, but my stepmom.

She glances at the suitcase on the bed behind me. "Need help unpacking?"

I shake my head. I'm spending the summer here in Plattsburgh, New York, with my dad, his new wife, and her daughter, Gracie. I've been here for only a day and a half, but I'm already counting down the days till I can go back to my mom's house in New York City. It's funny—I just moved into a house full of people, but somehow I feel as if I'm all on my own.

I miss my best friend, Stella. I miss my own room and my cat, Maggie. I miss pulling out my laptop and my cell phone whenever I want. Most of all, I miss my mom. She thought I should spend some time with my dad to get to know his new family, but I miss my *old* family—the way things were a couple of years ago when my mom and dad were still together. Why can't things just go back to the way they were?

My stepmom comes into the room and sees the jewelry I've laid out on the dresser. She "oohs" and "aahs" over a friendship bracelet that Stella made for me before I left. I can tell my stepmom is trying to be nice, but I'm just not in the mood for conversation.

"I have something that I think you might like," she says, her eyes hopeful. "I'll be right back."

As my stepmom leaves the room, five-year-old Gracie pokes her face through the doorway. "What're you doing?" she asks.

"Nothing," I mumble. Gracie has been glued to me ever since I got here. It's hard enough to share a room—complete with twin beds and pink princess bedspreads—but Gracie wants to share every waking *moment* with me.

I busy myself organizing the jewelry on my dresser. I reach for Stella's friendship bracelet and quickly slide it into my pocket, afraid that Gracie is going to see it and want to share that, too.

When my stepmom comes back, she dangles something in front of me. It's a necklace—a silver heart pendant on a chain. It must be a hundred years old, and it's not my style at all. I try not to make a face.

"My grandma gave me this when I was about your age," my stepmom says. "It helped me through a pretty tough time. Try it on and see if you like it."

She places the pendant in my hand and squeezes my shoulder. "Gracie and I are going to do some scrapbooking," she says. "Do you want to join us?"

"Um, not right now." I try not to sound rude.

I catch the flicker of disappointment in my stepmom's eyes. "Maybe later," she says, closing the door gently behind her.

As quiet settles over the room, I check the clock. 3:52. I wonder what Stella's doing right now.

I sigh, stretch out on the bed, and examine the pendant. It has a hinge along the left side of the heart. Is it a locket? I slide my thumbnail down the groove on the other side and try to open it, but it won't budge.

I reach for a nail file and try to pry the locket open. Just as I'm about to give up, I hear a *pop*. The now-open locket springs from my hand and disappears over the edge of the bed.

Scooting forward on my stomach, I peer over the side of the bed and reach for the locket. It's empty— no photos, no secret messages, no nothing. But as my fingers close around the locket, I feel my stomach drop. Something shifts beneath me, and then I'm falling. I squeeze my eyes shut, bracing for impact. I wait—one second, two, three—much too long for such a short fall. When I finally hit the floor, I feel a sharp pain in my temple. *Ouch!* Did I hit the dresser?

As I reach for my forehead, my hand brushes against something rough—not carpet, but something strangely familiar: *grass.* I open my eyes to a field of green, blinking against the blinding sunlight.

My temple throbs as I sit up. The world spins around me. I take a deep breath, a breath filled with the scent of lilacs. I glance over my shoulder at a long row of green bushes bursting with purple flowers. I'm sitting beside a lilac hedge on a broad lawn. Behind me, a tunnel through the hedge leads to another yard. Across the lawn is the back of an enormous gray house, several stories tall with a tower on top.

I hear the *creak* of a door hinge. I crawl through the tunnel and peer through the leaves at the house. A sour-faced woman steps onto the porch. She's wearing a long, old-fashioned skirt and apron, and her brown hair is pulled back into a tight bun. Behind her, a dark-haired girl skips out onto the porch and down the steps into the backyard. When I see what she's wearing, I suck in my breath. Her fancy pink dress has delicate lace trim, and her wide sash is tied in an enormous bow. These two seem to have walked straight out of the pages of a history book.

As the girl steps into the yard, my heart races. She's walking right toward me. I shrink back into the tunnel, not sure if I want her to see me or not.

She perches on a wooden swing hanging from a tree branch no more than three feet away. She looks friendly and curious, her brown eyes shining. *Who is she?* I wonder. She looks like someone I'd like to meet.

"Mind you keep your dress tidy, Miss Samantha," the woman calls from the porch.

Now I know the girl's name: *Samantha.*

Suddenly, there's a sharp tug on my foot. Some-one—or some *thing*—is trying to pull me backward into the tunnel!

I yank my foot away and whirl around to get a look at my attacker—a redheaded boy with a snub-nosed face. He's on his hands and knees, peering through the tunnel from the yard next door.

"Hey!" he says in an accusatory tone. "What were you doing in there?"

Author's Note

I had fun imagining Samantha and Nellie's trip
to Paris in 1907. While researching this mystery,
I studied tourist guides from the early 1900s
and read many current sources. But this story is
fiction, and for the sake of the mystery, I've used
artistic license in describing tourist sites—and
how they might have appeared to visitors more
than a century ago.